This book is dedicated to my little sister Glenda,

I love you blackie

DYSFUNCTIONAL

BILLIE DUREYA SHELL

DYSFUNCTIONAL

Front Cover Image By graphic designer Billie Dureyea Shell & Kenny Writes

First Printing Edition 2021

ISBN 978-1-7350234-7-2

ACKNOWLEDGEMENT

First and foremost I have to give honor to My Lord And Saviour Jesus Christ without him now of this would be possible. 2020 was a MUTHA FUCCA Corona Virus made shit hard 4 niggas but we made it threw y'all keep your head up and know that God got us, no matter they throw in our way no one can stop what God has plan for you...
Its 2021 now FUCC 2020 and Covid 19.... Now to my family momma I love you and you no I got you no matter what. You mean the world 2 me oh and NO MORE PINCHING LOL. To my little sister Glenda I love you blackie, you No I Got You always

To my Wife Shatoya Shell you get on my damn nerves 🙎
but I wouldnt trade you 4 anything In the world I love ❤
you more then words can ever express. To all my children 👫
I love y'all Jazmine, Ant'Tuan, Davon, Anthony, David,
Lil Dureyea, Alura, Queen Diavion, Cameron,
Preniece, Shaniece and Tajh I love u all and I'll 4ever have ur
back you all give me a reason 2 smile... to my cousin Zane RIP
nigga I miss u more then anyone will ever no, your always
remembered love you bro. to my cousin Ty I miss you thank 4
looking out 4 me and Zane you played a big part in my life
and I always looked up to you I love you... Uncle Woody I
miss you and love you, you no your my favorite uncle... To my
nigga Jamal love you, my brothers Lawrence and fred thank 4
showing me the game I love yall 4 that. To my oldest sister
Nedra love you thank you 4 always having my back. to my
family uncles anties cousins etc.. I love y'all even those of you
that act funny as fuck

To my dark side niggas y'all no what it is YAAH GANG....
Now to all my readers and fans I love you thanks for reading I
hope u enjoy this book as much as I enjoy writing
them with this Corona Virus 19 shit there ain't shit to do but
write so I'm on my shit with that being said y'all be safe cover
your face and love each other life is short so love the ones that
really love I'm gone no. enjoy the book

STAY SAFE

Author Billie Dureyea Shell
THERE'S NOTHING U CANNOT DO
IF U PUT UR MIND 2 IT.
All you nigga's got EDD money so aint no excuse
why you can't get a book LOL

Chapter One

KATIE

"I do . . . I do! . . . I-do . . ." I practiced my I do's in the mirror until my voice went hoarse, and I didn't plan on stopping anytime soon. I'm not going to let a little strain on my vocal cords bother me, so I kept right on practicing. "Hago eso!" That's I do in Spanish. "I do." I smiled at the image in the mirror as she smiles back at me. "I do . . ." Uh-oh there goes another I do along with what was left of my tired voice, but laryngitis is the least of my worries. Come to think of it I don't have any worries at all. My life is absolutely perfect. Well, perfect if I could erase the fact that I flunked out of law school, or hide my two failed, very embarrassing attempts to become a licensed chiropractor. Did I mention how embarrassing that was? Then there is the teeny tiny little issue of me turning thirty next month without a degree. Ugh, now why did I have to go and bring that up? Usually, when I think of my failed college education, I go into my woe is me faze, but that wouldn't be necessary, not today anyway. My life is finally on track. Excuse me; my love life is finally on track. I'm still turning thirty without a degree. I shouldn't let that bother me, though, right? It's just a piece of paper. Why do people make such a big deal about it? A degree doesn't make me any less of a woman. I think if I keep telling myself that long enough, I might actually start believing it . . . Not! Truth be told, I will not be satisfied with myself until I pass the bar. My father always said, "Katie," that's me, "determination without hard work means nothing." Now, Daddy never took the time to explain to me what it meant when you worked hard, had the drive, determination, a good education, and still ended up a failure. I'll try to forget the unsuccessful portion of my life for now because I'm about to marry the man of my dreams, Doctor Eric Reynolds. In less than two weeks, June seventh, after the priest announces us, husband and wife, I'll be Mrs. Dr. Eric Reynolds. That has a nice ring to it. Speaking of rings, I blush as I look down at my hand to face the yellow gold, pear-shaped 5.98-carat engagement ring Eric placed on my finger that sparkles against my porcelain skin like glass out in the middle of the sea. Once I showed off the new rock I was wearing my girlfriends, and sisters were all blown away by Eric's ring choice, as was I. He has impeccable taste were the words that came tumbling out of my resentful sister Kyle's mouth when she laid eyes on my ring. That night, when Eric and I announced our engagement, I could see the jealousy burning in Kyle's pale face. That green-eyed monster almost swept her away right in front of us. She wished she had my life—she wanted it all for herself. I could tell she wants what Eric and I have so she could be the one about to marry a gorgeous, distinguished, wealthy doctor. I wanted so desperately bad to pat her on the back and tell her the love of her life was waiting for her right around the corner, but why lie? I don't believe that, and neither will she. Kyle knew she would never have a man like my Eric. He's successful, handsome, strong, a good provider, and has all of his own teeth. What would he, a well-to-do dentist, want with a woman like my thirty-four-year-old unemployed sister? Kyle has nothing going for herself, although there is one thing she has that makes me a little envious of her: a college degree. She has one of those online degrees, so I guess I really don't envy her at all. What a loser! Kyle reminds me of Kim Zolciak from The Real Housewives of Atlanta. Like Kim, Kyle is extra loud, boisterous, obnoxious, rude, and she has a bad false sense of self. The only good thing about my sister is she's not like Kim Zolciak grabbing for a microphone to force her un-God given talent on us. Well, not anymore, that is. Lo-ser. Then there is my little sister Epiphany. She's the youngest of us three. She's the polar opposite of Kyle. I could actually stay in the same room with Epiphany longer than five minutes without a sudden urge to strangle her. Epiphany looks up to me, still obeys whatever I say, and she doesn't cross me. I like that in a woman. She's also easygoing, soft-spoken, and knows exactly when to shut up. She even can offer up some good old fashion, sound advice at times. And you know, I find myself listening at times. Epiphany doesn't have a degree either. I guess she planted somewhere in the back of her mind she would retire from being a bank teller when she's old and gray. Now, I think the only thing more pathetic than a twenty-six-year-old bank teller is a woman who would take the time and hang an online college degree on her wall for the world to see. Both of them are such losers! Then there's me: Kate Lynn Morgan. I would consider myself the sane one out of us three with a wonderful life. I'm everything I dreamt I would be. Just getting married at twenty-nine and childless wasn't exactly in the plans, but hey, better late than never. I would like to believe that too, but I don't. I thought I would be married at twenty-one, have my first child at twenty-three, pass the bar at twenty-five, and be ready for early retirement at forty. My life didn't quite work out that way, but I think I still have it going on. Some might even say I'm the total package. I'm intelligent with a great body and perfect skin. I have natural blonde shoulder-length hair, and a nice new set of boobs I bought and paid for last summer. I stand 5-foot-7 and weigh one hundred thirty-one pounds. I'm everything a man would want in a wife, so why did it take Eric Reynolds so long to find me? One afternoon, I was patiently waiting in line at the library to check out some books when I spotted him standing two people ahead of me. I could smell his cologne from my position in line. It was either his scent or one of the two old ladies that separated us. I knew it wasn't either of those hags; it was him. He was wearing a Marc Jacobs fragrance. I couldn't make out exactly which one, but he smelled so good—good enough for me to knock down the two old ladies and get a little closer, but I knew that thought would pass. And it did. All I was interested in was going back home, eat over half of the cookie dough ice cream in my freezer, and cuddle up with a good book, maybe two. That's not what I really wanted to do, but I had no other options. I didn't exactly have a parade of gentleman callers lined up waiting for me. But little did I know, after a visit to the local library, I wouldn't need a parade of gentleman callers, because now I would have just one. The right one: Eric Reynolds. No middle name, just Eric. He said, "Hello there," when I exited the library through the automatic sliding doors. At that point, I didn't know if he was waiting for me or if he was just standing there. I didn't ask because I didn't care. Yes, I did! As I stood there looking up at him, my heart skipped beats as the fading sun melted into his golden-brown skin. My mind instantly started to race. I was no longer interested in any of the novels I planned on finishing that night. I could've cared less about the main characters, the plots, or the endings. This man, now standing right in front of me, snatched my attention and held it hostage. After he introduced himself with, "My name is Eric Reynolds," he repeated his first name and then spelled it out for me: "Eric, E-R-I-C." I thought that was kind of odd, but I didn't question him; my mind was too occupied on what to say next. I thought about, "Hi, I'm Katie," but settled on the second thing that came to my mind, which was, "Good for you, Eric Reynolds." I read in Cosmo coy is the new black. I have to remind myself to cancel my subscription. My next reaction was to say something else before he walked away with a look of defeat on his face, but I didn't have to worry about that because he didn't walk away. He cracked a smile and said . . . uh . . . aw hell, I don't remember what he said next. His smile, those dimples, the small cleft that rested at the bottom of his chin—his strong voice, his dark bedroom eyes... everything about him already had me mesmerized, so I had to know more. I wasn't about to let him leave. Not now. Not yet. Not without my phone number. My e-mail address. My shoe size. Ring size. Something! I was on fire for the handsome stranger, but I kept my cool. Something else I read in Cosmo. Maybe I won't cancel my subscription, after all. "My name is Katie." I wouldn't dare say, Kate. "Katie, huh . . ." His eyes pointed toward the plastic bag I was holding. "Carl Weber, James Patterson, F. Scott Fitzgerald." He started rambling off the authors in my bag one by one. "I see you're really into the fiction novels." At that moment, I felt so silly. I wasn't planning to read Employment Law for Business by Dawn D. Bennett-Alexander and Laura P. Hartman when I left the library. It was clear I wasn't going to be up late, refreshing my memory on the black-letter rules the same as I'd done the night before the bar exam. I didn't have anything of substance in my bag. My reading material consisted of nothing but colorful make-believe, so I lied. "I'm just taking it easy tonight." I winked at him when I said, "Lawyers need a night off too, you know." I lied big time! I quickly switched the conversation without leaving him any more time to probe. I asked, "Where are your selections?" "Actually, I just came to the library to do a little research." I didn't bother to ask what he was researching; I was too busy staring into his beautiful mouth. Behind his full lips sat thirty-two of the most perfect teeth I've ever seen. Right then and there, he popped the question. There was no more small talk. No more flirting. He just did it. He asked, "Katie, will you . . ." I thought this is it! My heart was on overload. I'd been waiting to hear these words my entire life. I wanted to leap into his arms and show him my gratitude for choosing me, but all I could say was, "I do!" That's when he looked at me. He grinned when he asked, "What did you just say?" As I'm standing there panting for air—and trying to think of a valid retraction to my foolish outburst—Eric popped the question again. "Katie, will you . . . have dinner with me?" Well, it wasn't the marriage proposal I thought I heard fall from his luscious lips, but it was a start. In that instant, I could see myself carrying this man's baby. Make that babies, as in more than one—more than ten if he wanted me to. I wondered if that is what love, at first sight, feels like. I thought about phoning Epiphany and asking her opinion, but not before I accepted Eric's dinner request. I had to say something fast and not another I do. I calmed myself and felt an easy "Sure" evaporate from somewhere inside of me. I said sure even though I really wanted to say, "I do" because I did. I already loved this man. I think he felt it too because we've been inseparable ever since. That was twelve months ago. I confessed to Eric the night he proposed to me that I fell in love with him right there at the library. I also confessed I wasn't really a lawyer. I love Eric even more now and was more than ready to become his wife. "I do . . ." I started practicing again. My day had to be perfect. My gown, my hair, my makeup, my wedding, and my I do's. I wouldn't allow anything to go wrong. I had the perfect man, at the perfect time and our lives will be perfect together . . .

Chapter Two

COURTNEY

"Courtney, please come out here so I can see how you look." That was my best friend Shaun—5-feet-11, light brown skin, slim, short black hair—who doubles as my wedding coordinator. He's the best wedding coordinator out on the west coast, so his flights to and from Los Angles were on me. His trips, his dining, his lavished hotel suites, and his wardrobe were always on me. I never understood why Shaun needed a new outfit each time he came back to Baltimore, nor did I find time to ask—I just went with the flow. Thank God for American Express! He waited not so patiently on the other side of the curtain in the boutique for me to come out wearing what I planned to walk down the aisle in. I decided against white. I'm not a ho, but I'm not the Virgin Mary either. "Courtney, what's taking you so long?" That was Shaun again. He was really starting to agitate me in the worse way. I had enough on my mind to think about like getting married in a month. My body tingles every time I think about it. Last year, I never thought I would be planning my wedding after meeting the man of my dreams. The tingles in my body are starting to turn into nausea. I loovvee Erik and all, but marriage? I'm not so sure I'm ready. Instead of giving in to my doubts, I stood up straight as I took deep breaths. I smiled at myself in the full-length mirror in the dressing room as I felt nausea suddenly leave my stomach. Cream, or eggshell, as Shaun would say, was most definitely my color. My hand landed on my stomach as I sized myself up. I stand an even 5-foot-5, golden brown skin, soft natural features, dark eyes, and even darker hair. As I start to turn my tight body from side to side to look at myself from all angles, Shaun's voice was getting louder. "Courtney, please!" He was getting frustrated, and he had good reason to be. This was the fourth boutique we'd been in, and the tenth ensemble that I'm sure I would decline to wear. I wasn't walking down the aisle in just any old thing. Everything . . . every single detail had to be perfect on this day. If I didn't feel like the beautiful center of attention that I planned to be, everything would be a disaster. "Courtney Byrd, if you don't come out here right now, I'm coming in there after you. Don't have me get put out of this place." I laughed almost aloud, listening to Shaun gripe on the other side of the curtain. "Byrd, I'm waiting." God, it annoyed the hell out of me when Shaun called me Byrd. My last name, Byrd, sounded so country, but that's who I am: Courtney Byrd. I'm a twenty-four-year-old successful college graduate. I attended Yale University, graduating at the top of my class with a master's degree in business back in two thousand seventeen. I'm currently a loan officer at Citizens Bank until Fenmore's opens. Fenmore's will be an upscale tapas bar right in the heart of Baltimore, hopefully opening by next fall. So far, my life is on point all the way down to the man of my dreams I mentioned earlier. His name is Erik Reynolds. He has become my heart and soul. Sometimes I think I was placed on this earth to love, honor, and cherish that man. Erick is so fine and tall—6-foot-3—and a lean one hundred seventy pounds. He has short, black hair, full lips, sexy bedroom eyes, a six-pack, and a big thang. He's probably the best lover I've ever had. He's successful, too. Erik is a practicing dentist in and out of Baltimore. He and I met at the supermarket one night right before closing time. I was craving pistachio nuts; fresh pistachio nuts that is. Not that shelved Planters garbage, so I put on my Prada flip-flops, some running pants, a white tank, and I was out the door. I let the top down on my candy apple red Camaro as Beyoncé came blaring out of the factory sound system the second I started the engine. I sang right along with Bey, not missing a single word. Was I in tune? Probably not, but that didn't stop me. Once I got to the market, I headed to the candy counter for my weekly dosage of my crunchy, oh-so-tasty drug. As I'm switching up to the register to pay for my peanuts, there he was in the self-checkout lane. Oh my God, I thought he was so sexy. My bottom lip sucked into my mouth without my permission, so I rapidly pushed it back out. I stole another fast glance, but quickly brushed him off. I see good-looking men all the time, but that didn't mean I could take one of them home with me. Lord knows I wanted to take this one home, though, but he was gone. By the time I retrieved my receipt from the machine, he was nowhere in sight. I didn't sweat it. I was heading back out to my car for a repeat performance of Beyoncé without a care in the world. As soon as the night air graced my skin, there he was . . . the guy from the checkout line. Aw, he was so gorgeous. Skip gorgeous, he was fine! Like Lance Alonzo fine. I breezed past him, hoping with all my strength, he would stop me. "Excuse me." I thought he couldn't be talking to me; I wouldn't be so lucky. When I turned to him, he was looking right at me, I thought waiting to ask for a lighter or something, so I didn't get my hopes up. I answered, "Yes?" but that was all I could say. I was captivated by this man. I tried to fight the feeling, but I could barely control myself. He wasn't fine; he was beautiful. Just my type, but I was sure all he wanted was a lighter or something silly like that, so I swiftly dismissed my visual fantasies. "I'm sorry to bother you." Was he serious? He wasn't bothering me. He was just what the doctor ordered. When he came closer, I clutched the bag in my hand. I thought, shit! My pepper spray was in the glove box of my car. I thought If I made a run for it, I could probably grab it before he grabbed me and my wallet. I didn't run though. I didn't want to run. I just stood there as he came closer. He was now standing right in front of me. Now I was sure he was about to ask for a light, but he didn't. He smiled at me and said, "I'm Erik Reynolds." I thought it was so cute the way he spelled out his first name, E-R-I-K. "Hi, I'm Courtney." We stood there in silence; our quiet stares colliding like two freight trains in the midst of the night. I didn't know what else to say, and, apparently, he didn't either because he just looked at me almost as if he was sizing me up. I thought, was he? No, he couldn't have been. I dismissed that thought even faster than I did that nonsense of taking him home. "It's a nice night." He was still smiling at me, so I smiled back when I said, "It sure is." I thought, should I have said that? I wanted to be cute and smooth. I read somewhere coy is the new black. He looked at me. "You look nice and comfortable." "Thank you. I just ran out for some nuts." I was so embarrassed. Erik blushed ever so lightly when he said, "Oh, really?" Right then, instead of asking for a lighter, Erik Reynolds asked me out to dinner. I couldn't believe this was happening right here in front of the market I frequent at least twice per week. And I would be in sweats and flip-flops. I prayed my toes were polished. I sighed relief when I looked down to see the fresh, clear coat glaring back at me. Thank goodness. Twelve months later, we're engaged to be married, and I couldn't be happier. Erik is everything I've ever dreamt of. He reminds me a lot of my father; Lord rest his soul. I love my daddy, and he loved me too, he just didn't accept me or my choices. See, I come from an old fashion, southern black family where being gay is anything but accepted. I did mention I'm a guy, right? Well, anyway, some say my father died of a broken heart because his only child, Courtney Michael Byrd III, is gay. I love who I am, and I've never tried to hide my sexuality from anyone, including my father. I don't exactly shout it from the rooftops, but I'm me, and I'm happy. And for the record, my dad died because he smoked two packs of cigarettes per day and drank a fifth of whatever he could get his hands on the quickest. He didn't wither away from a broken heart over his gay son or his failed marriage to my mother. Puhleease! He killed himself. Well, Jack Daniels and Newport 100's killed him, but that's a different story for a different day. Shaun gasped when I appeared from behind the curtain. I think I even saw a tear spiral from behind his blue contacts. "Let me look at you." He admired the cream, excuse me, the eggshell suit I had on. I looked at him when I said, "This is it. This is the one I want." He was happy, and so was I. I had finally chosen the perfect suit. The wedding was less than a month away, June twenty-fourth, and I surely couldn't show up in my tank, sweatpants, and flip flops. Now, everything was set. I was all ready to marry Erik and start our new lives together . . .

Chapter Three

KATIE

Well, the time has finally come. The day I've dreamt of my entire life was here at last. I was about to become Mrs. Dr. Eric Reynolds. I loved the sound of that. I couldn't wait to get my new checks in the mail with my new name printed right above my new address. Eric and I are moving out to Howard County. It's a quiet little suburb of Baltimore. I'm a city girl myself. "Hold still." That was my little sister, Epiphany—5-foot-2, short, black bob, and chunky. She was standing over me doing my makeup. I kept her and my mother close to me just in case I needed a little support even though I knew I would be fine. I was born to be a bride, unlike my two sisters. Speaking of sisters, I'm so glad, Kyle—5-foot-8, blonde, pale white, plumped lips, and liposuctioned all over—was nowhere in sight. I couldn't stand to look at her or her wigs today, so I made sure she stayed nice and busy far away from me. It made her feel important that I gave her so much to do on my special day. She would probably be crushed if she knew I kept her busy to make sure she stayed out of my way. I didn't want any of her bitterness, awkwardness, or man hating-ness to rub off on me. Not today, anyway. This day was all about me, me, me. Not her or her botched boob job or caked-on foundation. I laughed to myself, thinking of just how hateful I can be at times, but who cares? It wasn't like I was saying any of these harsh words to her face. Now don't get me wrong, I plan to say all of what I'm thinking to her and more, but just not today. I'll let her think her imperfections went unnoticed for the next twenty-four hours. "Epiphany, I don't want to look like Kyle. Pleaseeee don't make me look like Kyle." Epiphany chuckled as she continued to run the makeup brush over my already flawless face. "Katie, just relax." Once Epiphany finally finished, she took a few steps back to admire her work. "You look beautiful." I turned and looked at myself in the mirror. Perfect! My dress, my hair, my skin . . . all of it was simply perfect, and I couldn't wait for Eric to see me coming down the aisle. He'll probably want to rip off my thirty-five hundred-dollar Vera Wang gown and take me right there on the altar. He finds me irresistible, and really, I can't blame him. I gave myself a wink in the mirror as I thought, if I were him, I would marry me too. I'm the lucky one, though. Whoever said, A good man is hard to find, was not joking! It seems like all the guys I've ever come across were either too old, too young, too gay, too married, or locked up for too long to make me happy. But not my Eric—he's just right for me. No, actually he's perfect for me and today, he's going to make me his wife, so we'll be perfect together.

Chapter Four

COURTNEY

"Courtney, seriously, you're shaking. Girl, you have to try and calm down." I wanted to haul off and slap Shaun. First of all, why does he insist on calling me, girl? I'm not a girl, and neither is he. We don't look like girls; we don't act like girls—at least I don't. We don't smell like girls, nor do we want to be girls. At least I don't. We're men. Two gay men, but yet every other word out of his mouth is girl this, or girl that. He's been flamboyant and over the top like that since we met in junior high, and that annoys the hell out of me! After my rant about Shaun and his gay slang, I tried to calm my nerves, but it wasn't happening. Mama always said I'd have days like this, but she never prepared me for my wedding day. I don't pray. I'm not spiritual whatsoever. I believe there is a Higher Power, but that's it. I don't drop to my knees every night and recite some repetitious bible verse, but I sure wish I had. Maybe a little prayer would help me now. I'll try it . . . Our Father which art . . . uh . .

. our Father . . . What am I doing? Hell, I don't know how to pray! Maybe I need a drink. Yeah, that's it! A bottle will make everything all better. "Shaun, can you make a run for me really quick?" I reached for my designer wallet to hand him however much money he needed. Hopefully, he won't need a new outfit just to run to the store. But if he did, as long as he could bring me something to calm me down, I will be more than happy to oblige. I need something strong; preferably tequila or . . . or . . . maybe whiskey will work better. Jameson should do the trick. When I looked at Shaun ready to reveal my foolish wish, he stopped me. "Put away your wallet and relax. Girl, you will be fine." There he goes again with that girl nonsense again. "Look at me." I didn't. "Courtney, look-at-me." Did I really have to look at him to hear him? I'm not deaf, you know. When we finally made eye contact, Shaun said, "You'll be fine. Erik loves you, and you love him. This is just a ceremony. It'll be over before you know it, and then the two of you can start your lives together. Byrd, all the people that love you are here right by your side to celebrate this very special day with you and Erik, so there is nothing for you to be worried about." Shaun is right, so why am I tripping out? Just listening to him is starting to soothe me a little, but I still needed that drink, though. "You are about to have the life people like me only dream about. Soon, you'll be opening your own business; you're marrying a man that most of your friends would kill to have, you're moving into a new home . . . Courtney . . . I-I just want what's best for you, and I believe Erik is what's best for you." I could tell he wanted to cry, but I'm glad he didn't. "Now, you go out there, and you take the man that you plan on spending forever with and leave all of your doubts and fears right here in this changing room." All I could do was hug Shaun because he was right, Erik is what's best for me. I love him more than I love myself, and I know he loves me even more. I never pictured myself getting married, but now I can't imagine myself not marrying Erik. We're going to have such a good life together, and it all starts today. The clock read three-fifty, so that meant it was time. I was expensively dressed and well-groomed. Now, if I could just get my nervous stomach out of my quivering kneecaps, I think I'll be okay. As Shaun and I head to the sanctuary, I took deep breaths just like I did the night I met Erik. When the double wooden doors opened, I took one last gasp of air and walked up to the man of my dreams.

Chapter Five

KATIE

"Epiphany, please be careful." My little sister was carrying in a family heirloom that I kept mounted in the small dining room at my old place. It wasn't actually an heirloom; more like a fairly expensive piece of crystal, my grandmother came across many years ago. Kyle asked, "So Katie, where is your new husband?" as she wrestled in the foyer with a box marked kitchen. Instead of offering to help her, I rolled my eyes up toward the vaulted ceiling. My skin crawls whenever Kyle mentions Eric, especially the way she says, husband. It sounds as if she drags every single letter out of her mouth one by one. Huuuussssssbbbaannddd. Ugh, I hated that with a passion. When I answered her, I made sure my voice was as sharp and aggravated as the look on my face. "Eric is away on business, Kyle. How many more times am I going to have to tell you that?" I thought, you stupid bitch! I didn't care how nasty I was to her. Maybe now she'll put down that box, grab her keys, and see herself out. I didn't want her in my new home anyway. She wasn't welcomed today, or ever. I should slap her silly for questioning my husband's whereabouts, but I'll try to keep it together for the time being. I promised Daddy I would. "Eric is always away on business; I'm surprised he even showed up at the wedding." Was this bitch serious? Can I help I married a doctor? I thought, of course, he has long hours, and he's never home. He's a doctor . . . He's-A-Fucking Doctor! I have to recite those words to myself every night to chase the anxiety away that keeps fizzing in the pit of my stomach. As I take bubble wrapping off the buddha statute, I start to feel ill. My head hurts; so does my stomach. I miss Eric so badly everything on my body aches, but it's okay . . . this is normal . . . I'm married to a doctor. That's why he isn't here. He's a doctor! When I feel the warm tears, I could no longer deny run down my pale face, I ran to the half-bath off the den. I wouldn't dare let either of my sisters see me cry. I couldn't let my weak side shine through. No way! I have a perfect life, not them. They didn't have anything. No husbands, no careers, no real education, nothing! I was the one they looked up to, so I had to keep it together even though I was breaking down at the seams because my husband isn't here. As hard as I wished that he was here, he isn't, and there was nothing I could do to change that. I need him so badly . . . I just want to look at him. Make love to him. Cuddle up next to him. I want to smell his breath. Listen to his voice call out my name. Oh God, I feel like I'm dying without my husband. I'm dying a slow, sick, agonizing death without him, but what could I do? He's gone, and I had to accept that. I had to face my fears head-on, which was I would be spending another night alone, all by myself. I married a doctor, so I'll probably be spending most of my days and nights just like this one—hunched over the toilet crying my eyes out. "Katie . . ." That was Epiphany calling me from the other side of the bathroom door after I bolted inside to get away from them. "Katie, sweetie, are you okay?" Her voice was calm and easy. I wanted to unlock the door, but I won't let her see me like this. Worst yet, I won't let Kyle see me like this. I'm a basket case. "Katie, open up." I'm sure she heard me whimpering when I called out, "I'm okay." I sniffled. "I'll . . . I'll be out in a minute." No, I'm not okay, and I'm never coming out of this bathroom, at least not until my husband comes home. I cried harder, thinking about Eric. I needed Epiphany and Kyle to leave so I could go upstairs and cuddle up in our bed with one of his nightshirts to smell the scent he left behind just for me. I shook my head as the tears continued. What was happening to me? I feel like I'm about to die right here on my knees. This is not the way I pictured my last few seconds on earth would be. "Katie, please let me in." I could hear Epiphany turn the gold doorknob back and forth trying to get to me, but I wasn't letting her in, and I'm not coming out. "Katie, open this door, right now!" Kyle? She had some nerve thinking I would let her in here. I'll die in this bathroom first, which is what I planned to do. "Katie Morgan, open this door. What is your problem? And why are you crying?" That's-it! I'm going to open the bathroom door long enough to slap the wind out of her. I'm sorry, Daddy. I stood up, grabbed some tissues to dry my wet, red face, adjusted by blouse back to its normal position, and unlocked the door to see my two evil sisters staring at me with their judgmental eyes and mouths full of disapproval. Now they're laughing at me . . . their bodies shook as their amusement erupted through my three-story home. Look at them; even Epiphany found humor in my despair. But she isn't laughing. Kyle wasn't either. "Katie, what's the matter?" That was Kyle trying her hardest to sound sincere. Trust me; it's an act. But before this goes any further, let me set these two bitches straight once and for all. "Epiphany, let me get something crystal clear with you, honey. I don't appreciate you budding into my business. That's number one!" "Katie, I was just making sure you were—" "NO! NO! NO!" I cut her off before she could finish because I didn't want to hear any of what she had to say. My finger waved at her as I shouted, "You are in my business so that you can run back to Mommy and Daddy with a full report of my life in tow." One down one to go. "And you." I glared over at Kyle. "How dare you question my husband's whereabouts?" "Katie, I wasn't—" "That's exactly what you were doing!" I cut her off, too. "And that's so unfair to me because I don't question either of you about your husbands, do I?" I looked at Epiphany. "Do I?" Then my eyes landed back on Kyle when I screeched, "DO I?!" much louder than the first time. "I don't question your husbands' whereabouts because neither of you has a husband for me to question. Both of you are just two lonely, single witches putting your pointy little noses where they don't belong." That will fix them. The next time I say leave me alone, they'll leave me the-hell-a-lone! I shot passed Kyle and Epiphany and headed for the staircase. I'm going to lock myself in our bedroom and wait for Eric. He'll be here soon, and when he does, everything will be perfect again.

Chapter Six

COURTNEY

"So, when are you guys planning to move into your new house?" That was Shaun sitting across from me in Starbucks. He decided to stay in Baltimore a few more weeks, and honestly, I'm happy he's here. Despite his over the top gay antics, I consider him one of my best friends. Since Shaun left Baltimore for LA, I've really missed him, so I enjoy any time we do get to spend together even if it's at my expense. On top of that, my wedding was absolutely fabulous because of him. The flowers, the decorations, the music, the seating—everything was on point. Just what I wanted, so I really didn't mind springing for a few extra weeks for him to stay. I took a sip of the strong coffee sitting in front of me before I answered Shaun. "The movers delivered the last of my things today; all of Erik's belongings have been at the new house for over a week." Shaun looked as if he was about ready to punch me. I was hoping he didn't because I was going to hit his ass right back, or at least reach for my pepper spray.

"Wait a minute . . . So you've been in that house all this time and didn't tell me?" Shaun waved his hand at me with attitude when he said, "Messy, messy, messy, Courtney Byrd, chile." "Shaun, I've been coming to your suite every day since you've been in Baltimore, so I guess it just slipped my mind." I tried to cover up the real reason why I didn't invite Shaun to our home. He just . . . He's always . . . Well, he didn't . . . Come to think of it, I really don't know why I haven't invited him to our new place yet. I guess I don't want to share Erick with him or anyone else right now. Our time is so limited together, and I just want him all to myself. I couldn't explain that to Shaun, though. Not right now, anyway. I can tell he was way too upset. "You sure have been coming to my suite every goddamn day. Every single day, Courtney, and it never once dawned on you to tell me you were moving?" I tried to lighten the mood. "Well, technically, I wasn't the one doing the moving. We hired Mayflower." "Courtney don't do that." Shaun didn't find my humor humorous. "You know what I meant. I've been there for you since the day you met Erik. I've been right here by your side whether I was in LA or camped out in a hotel here in Maryland, and you didn't even have enough decency to take me to the front lawn of your new house?" "Shaun, it just slipped my mind, okay?" "Hell no, it's not okay. I'm supposed to be your best friend, but yet you conveniently let it slip your mind that you moved into your new residence that I have yet to see? Courtney, I cannot believe you." It was clear Shaun was pissed at me. If it means anything, I wasn't trying to hurt his feeling. With so much going on, and Erik away on business, leaving me here to take care of everything, I got a little sidetracked. Erik was always flying to a new city or taking a train hundreds of miles away from home. Seminar after seminar this week, and who knows what the next week. It's tough being married to a traveling dentist. Since the wedding three weeks ago, I've probably seen Erik all of five times. I miss him more than anything, but I'm so busy at the bank, I don't really have that much time to ponder over his absences. With him being away, I try and stay focused on work and getting Fenmore's opened. As Shaun continues to curse the day I was born for not bringing him out to our new home, I start to think more and more about my husband. I wonder what he's wearing right now. What kind of cologne he has on? What color is his underwear? Does he have on any underwear? I take a deep breath as I feel my insides start to heat up. I bite down on my bottom lip as my thoughts of my husband start to pour into a fantasy. A rugged, nasty, downright porn-style fantasy. I've had to be gone away from the conversation with Shaun for at least ten minutes or so, but he is still going on, and on, and-on. I really wish he would accept my apology and shut up already. Besides, I only have one thing on my mind right now, and that's being with the love of my life. I think I'll text Erik just to let him know I'm thinking about him. On second thought, I'll send him a pic. I thought, how about this one? as I start scrolling through the photos of me in my cell. I'm going to send him the picture I took in our bed last night. After he gets it, maybe he'll call me so we can get nasty on Facetime. Or just perhaps, he'll hop on the next plane and come home from wherever he is so we can nasty in person. "Did you hear me, Courtney?" Send. My picture, along with a steamy little message was on its way to Erik's cell phone. I took another sip of my lukewarm coffee as I impatiently waited for Erik's response. Hopefully, he'll be telling me he's on his way home soon. I smile and take another sip from my cup as I look over at Shaun. It's obvious he's still pissed off. Now, is he still mad about the house thing, or has his anger flipped into rage because I haven't been listening to him? It didn't matter because all I could think of was Erik. I need him so bad right now, but in the meantime, I guess I'll tend to my best friend, and just maybe he'll forgive me and shut the hell up. I offer Shaun a smile when I ask, "Now, what were you saying?"

Chapter Seven

KATIE

I lie in bed, winded, worn out, and still trembling after welcome home sex with Eric. I wiped the sweat from my brow right before I reached for the bottle of water I placed on the nightstand. What do you know—empty! Eric surprised me last night when I heard his key jingle in the lock. I thought I was dreaming, so I didn't move. First, I heard him in the kitchen; then, his footsteps became closer as he headed up the staircase. I still didn't move. I felt paralyzed. Immobile. Motionless. I couldn't believe he was here. He said he wouldn't be home for another day or two, so I wasn't expecting him. Eric quickly entered our bedroom and headed right for me. Instead of a, "Hi, honey, I'm home!" he rushed my lifeless body as existence started pumping through me. I could breathe again because Eric was home. I could exhale now because I could touch him—feel his warm flesh that started crawling all over my body. My vagina released before he even entered me. I was so wet, my sex dripping for him. Eric plunged deep inside me as his big strong hands started strumming my frame. I was going wild. I couldn't control myself any longer, so I released down his shaft with his tongue stirring in and out of my mouth. He made love to me and didn't stop until I begged for mercy. As I sit here reminiscing about the passionate hours spent with Eric, I clutch our sheets close, listening to the shower water spray. I can just imagine his lean body bathing on the other side of the glass shower doors. My thoughts of joining him were interrupted by my cell phone that started buzzing. It was probably Kyle or Epiphany calling to apologize. I thought it's about time. I haven't spoken to either of them since my little bathroom breakdown over a week ago. When I reached for my phone, I could still hear vibration because It wasn't my phone buzzing, it was Eric's cell on the nightstand next to my empty water bottle. I laid my phone back down and picked his up. His screen told me he had a new picture waiting to be opened. The little mailbox on his screen was calling my name. I just had to open it to see who would be sending Eric a picture, especially this time of night. On second thought, I'm not going to invade his privacy. I'll just ask him about it when he gets out of the shower. As I'm holding his phone, it vibrated again. Another picture? Who the hell is this from? I exhaled. "What am I doing?" After I asked myself that question aloud, I cracked a smile at how foolish I was acting. Paranoid was more of the word. Eric has never shown me any signs of unfaithfulness, so I had nothing to worry about. Absolutely nothing to . . . be . . . Screw that! I had to open this picture mail. Second thought, maybe I shouldn't. What if it's just his Aunt Ollie from

Toledo sending him another family photo again? It's harmless, I thought until the third picture came through. Before I could catch myself, I tapped the screen where the mailbox flashed. Oh-my-God! I couldn't believe my eyes. What . . . why? . . . I was at a loss. I couldn't believe what I was seeing. Was his phone locked? I couldn't believe it. Why is Eric's phone locked? He's never locked his phone before. At least I don't think he has. I've never had a reason to go through his phone before now. I sigh before I placed his phone back down. It was just his Aunt or some other family member sending him something crazy. Probably another one of those chain picture text thingies'. I sat on the bed with my legs crossed. I tried to remain calm, but I couldn't. Why is his phone on vibrate? And locked? What is he hiding? Who is he hiding? I jumped up and headed for the bathroom door. I needed answers now! I didn't want to wait until his shower was over. I became furious! I was so upset I was shaking. I wanted to kill my husband. He was hiding something from me, and I wanted to know what. I had to know what. I had to see the pictures that were about to run us into divorce court and me into an insane asylum. I turned from the bathroom door and headed back for Eric's phone. I picked it up again, but the screen still read Locked. The second I touched the screen, it asked me for a passcode. I instantly started racking my brain, thinking, what could it be? I tried his birthday, 1-0-0-9-8-5, but that didn't work. I thought I'd try the year he was born, 1-9-8-5. No luck. Damnit! I tried our street address, 4-8-8-2. My old apartment street address, 1-2-1-4. I tried the last four of his social security number. My social security number. His shoe size. My shoe size. I'm running out of time and numbers, but I couldn't stop now. I had to see these pictures! I then tried the year we were married and still came up empty-handed. I tried the year we met . . . still nothing. Eric, what is it! I tried the last four digits of his cell number, our house phone number, then my cell number, but nothing worked. I'm locked out of my husband's cell, but I'm determined to get in. I'm going to crack this code if it's the last thing I do. I need to see these pictures! My intuitions were on overload. Something didn't feel right, and I was about to get to the bottom of it. What could this code be, Eric . . . what is your lock code, damnit! Right then, my thumb landed on 1-9-9-0, and that's when it happened: The screen unlocked. The year I was born, of course! I felt relieved and a little flattered that Eric would use my birth year as his passcode. I thought, aww that's so cute, but back to the matter at hand. That envelope was waiting for me, and I was more than ready to open it, but I didn't get a chance to because Eric was standing in the doorway of our bedroom, dripping wet with a towel wrapped around the lower part of his muscular body. I could see the look of anger in his eyes. He was livid just as I was a few seconds ago. His jagged voice stormed toward me when he yelled out, "Katie, what are you doing with my phone?!"

Chapter Eight

COURTNEY

"Well, I see it worked," I spoke softly as Erik lies behind me with his arms wrapped around my body. We just made mad passionate love for the second time. I missed him so much, and his body told me he missed me too. When he came home tonight, I felt almost as if my world had stopped and restarted from his first hello. God, I love this man. "You see what worked, Court?" "The pictures I sent you." "What pictures?" He looked confused. "The pictures I sent to your cell last night. You weren't due back from your trip until tomorrow night, but here you are right now, just like I knew you would be." I raised my head in his silence and looked over at my husband's vacant face as he stared back at me. "Erik? . . . I sent pics to your cell." Now I was starting to get agitated. I grabbed my phone off the charger next to my side of the bed and quickly retrieved one of the pics I sent him. It was me laying across our perfectly made bed stark-naked. When I handed Erik my phone, he looked at the picture as if it was the first time he'd seen my naked body. "Now, do you remember?" Before he could answer, I could hear his phone vibrating next to him. I looked away from Erik to peek over at the clock. I'm thinking, should I question him as to why his phone is ringing so late, or should I be more concerned as to why he's pretending it's not ringing at all? I chose door number one. "Erik, who would be calling you this late?" I'm not the jealous type, more so curious. I kicked myself after I asked him that question because I was setting myself up to hear something I didn't want to hear, possibly, but I wanted to know. I wanted to know, but I got nothing. Erik just stared at me as if I was speaking a different language. "Erik, who was that?" "How am I supposed to know?" Now I know he didn't call himself getting an attitude. "Well, if you looked at your . . ." I was cut off by the buzz of his phone again. "Don't you think you should get that?" My raised tone didn't faze him as he just laid there. "Well, since you don't want to answer it, I will." When I reached for Erik's phone, he grabbed me. His tight grip shook me. I didn't know what to do. What should I do? Yell? Scream for help? Call the police? Call Shaun? Call Mama? Was this going to turn physical? Was this a domestic dispute? My mind started to race as my husband's grip gripped tighter. Why is he doing this? Why had he become so angry? Was I out of line for wanting to know who was calling him at this hour? I became frightened. I didn't know what to do. What could I do? What should I do? I didn't have any answers, so the tears started. Why am I crying? Why am I letting my weak side come out? Does he think I'm weak? If he does think I'm weak, will he leave me? Pull it together, Courtney! I tried to coach myself through this, but I didn't know where to start. My heart was pounding, hoping Erik would let me go. Then my heart started pounding even harder, hoping he wouldn't. I didn't want him to leave me. This was our first fight since we've been together, and I was becoming unglued. He better say something fast, or I was going to lose it. I had already lost it. I was crying uncontrollably. Nonstop. This wasn't just a few tears here and there. No, no. As Oprah would say, this was an ugly cry. I wish Oprah were on right now. Maybe she could tell me what to do. Perhaps tell me what I did wrong. "Erik, please, you're hurting me." "Why are you crying?" We started speaking at the same time. He asked again, "Courtney, why are you crying?" "You're . . . you're hurting me, Erik." My whimpering voice was just above a whisper. He released me right before he apologized. "I'm sorry. I shouldn't have grabbed you." I dried the water from my chin as he stared into my eyes. Oh my God, I'm sure I look a mess. Hopefully, he doesn't think so. Just as I was pulling myself together, his phone started ringing again. Who was trying so hard to get in contact with him? "Erik, who is that?" I wasn't crying anymore. My voice became sharp. I needed answers, and I needed them now. "You know what Courtney, here . . ." He hit the red ignore button on his screen before he held the power button to turn the phone off. "Are you happy now? The phone is off, problem solved!" He got up and headed for the bathroom. "Erik, you still didn't answer my question! Who would be calling you back to back at this hour?" He turned to me. "Courtney, I'm a doctor, okay. I get calls about patients at all hours of the night; you know that. I didn't answer the call because I was trying to have some alone time with you. We haven't seen each other in almost a week, so whoever was trying to reach me could wait!" Ugh, now I feel so bad. I caused this huge scene over nothing. Erik was just trying to spend some time with me, and I went and ruined it. Now, I have to make this right before this foolish fight goes any further. Would an I'm sorry be enough? I'll try it. "I'm sorry, Erik. I really am. You know I'm not like that." I repeated it. "I'm sorry . . ." It wasn't enough. I could tell he was still upset with me. "Why don't you come back to bed?" He didn't respond. Instead, he turned and headed for the bathroom. "Erik?" He stopped in his tracks, but he never turned toward me. "Courtney, . . . I need to take a shower." "Why are you in such a rush to take a shower?" When he finally faced me, I wish he hadn't. His eyes pierced right through me. Thank God looks couldn't kill; if they could, Shaun would be planning me a fashionable, fabulous, flawless funeral. "Courtney, I'm taking a shower because I'm dirty. We made love twice tonight, so I need to rinse some of the sex off my body before I go to bed. Is that okay with you?" I didn't reply. If I say anything, I'm sure I would burst out into tears again, and I didn't want that to happen, so I just let him go. I stayed glued to the spot on the bed until I heard the shower start. I was relieved our first argument was over. I was ready to close my eyes, pretend none of this happened, and just go to sleep. And that's exactly what I planned to do, but before I could lie my head down on the pillow, there was a burst of light that started shining inside our bedroom. It was Erik's phone. I thought he turned it off, but obviously, he didn't; he just switched it to silent. I looked at the bathroom door, then back down to the phone. I thought, who was trying so hard to get in touch with him and why? When I grabbed the phone, I noticed he had a new voicemail message waiting to be heard. Without delay, I tapped the envelope ready to find out who was trying so hard to get in contact with my husband, but what do you know . . . LOCKED!

Chapter Nine

KATIE

I awakened alone in our bed to the sound of the flock of happy birds chirping outside the window. I knew my husband wasn't lying next to me, but I still ran my hand over his side of the bed. He hadn't come home last night. He hadn't come home or taken any of my phone calls. A single tear escaped from my eye as I lay here alone watching the sun peek over the horizon. This is supposed to be the happiest time of my life, but it's turned out to be the lowest point I've ever seen. Maybe I should call my sisters since I haven't spoken to either of them in over a month. On second thought, I'm not calling them. They'll only make fun of me and say, "I told you so!" More tears followed the one that ran fugitive as I sat up and reached for my phone so that I could call Epiphany. I can confide in her—tell her what's really going on with me and my marriage. She won't judge me. She won't say, "I told you so!" She won't laugh and talk about me behind my back.

Then again, maybe I should call Kyle. Scratch that thought! She'll definitely judge me, talk behind my back, laugh in my face, and scream, "I told you so!" from every rooftop in Baltimore. I'll just call home, so Daddy can come and get me. I can stay with him and Mom until I get on my feet. Anything is better than sitting in this big house all alone, missing Eric. I just can't take it anymore, so I'm leaving . . . I picked up my phone, ready to dial until I hear the garage door cables. The next thing I knew, Eric was standing in the bridge of our bedroom door looking at me. I could see in his eyes he had something to say, but he didn't speak. He was probably waiting for me to start flipping out on him for not answering any of my calls last night, the way I flipped out on him about his locked, vibrating cell phone; and why the mysterious pictures were deleted before they were ever opened. Maybe he was waiting for me to run to the bathroom and cry some more. Whatever Eric thought I would do, I didn't. I just sat there in the bed that we were supposed to share last night, silent. "Good morning." That was it. He had nothing else to say. No explanations as to why he couldn't answer his phone when I called him last night or where he's been. I got nothing but a casual 'good morning.' "Hello, Eric." My voice cracked. I wanted to ask him where he's been or why he ignored my phone calls, texts', and voice mail messages, but I didn't bother; I just can't with the excuses today. His deep tenor voice asked, "How'd you sleep last night?" "Alone." I looked away from him and turned my nose up. "I'm always alone, Eric. Always here by myself unable to be with you . . .

hell, I can't even get you on the phone. I'm-I'm tired of this. I can't take it anymore." When I started to cry, he sprinted over to me. "Don't touch me!" I blocked all of his advances. "I need you more than a couple of nights per week. You are my husband, not my boyfriend. You're not some booty call. I need you, Eric . . . not just sometimes . . . Not just Tuesdays and Thursdays or whenever you decide to come home. I need a full-time husband, Eric! Not-not this . . . not you because you're never here." "Katie, baby, I love you. I don't want to see you like this." I flinched when he smoothed a strain of my hair out my face. "Listen, babe, I know my schedule is hard on you, and I'm sorry. Everything I'm doing, I'm doing for us. I promise I'll do better, though, Katie. You'll see. I promise it won't always be like this." I stopped fighting him off and let him hold me. I let him dry my tears. I allowed myself to fall into his embrace as he kissed my lips. His touch was so soft and gentle. His caress was comforting. I know I shouldn't be letting my guard down for him because nothing is going to change, but I can feel myself slipping right where he wants me to be. I should be making the call to my parents, but instead, I'm giving in to my husband as if his penis was going to make everything all better. I already knew once we made love, he'll be gone, and I'll be left all alone wondering when he's coming back. I should be stronger, not giving in, but I can't help myself. My tears stopped as my nipples became erect. I wanted Eric to put them into his mouth one after the other. I wanted to feel his strong hands on my ass. I wanted him to look me in the eyes and tell me he loves me and only me. I wanted him to want me. I wanted his body to desire mine as much as mine desired his. I wanted to feel every inch of his manhood inside of me. I wanted him to make love to the pit of my soul. I'm on fire. He is too. I could tell. I shivered from his rugged hands that were all over me. He had me under some type of hypnotic spell, causing goose pimples to line my bare skin from his scent. My va jay jay was about to explode from anticipation as he leaned into me. I can feel my climax about to rush from my body. "Make love to me, Eric." My nails clawed up his back. "I want you inside of me." "Oh yes, baby, but I need to take a shower first." I said, "No, you don't," before kissing his full lips. "Take me right here, Eric. I don't want to wait any longer. I can't go another minute without you." "Let me shower first, Katie, and then I'll be all ready for you." When he stood up, so did I. "Where do you think you're going? Huh . . . I finally have some time with you, and you're running off to take a shower?" When his eyes racked away from mine to the floor, I asked him, "Where were you last night?" He didn't answer me. "Who were you with? What were you doing? And don't tell me work. Don't tell me what you've been telling me because I'm tired of hearing it! You come in ready to rush right to the shower as if you're trying to scrub yourself clean, but of what? Of whom, Eric?" I pulled my short, white silk robe closed, waiting for him to answer me. "Katie, you already know I'm working, so don't do this. Don't place doubts in your head about me because you know there is not another woman on this earth for me." I don't want to hear this. I don't want to hear another I'm working excuse. God, I hate him so much right now. I swopped my hair behind my ear as I contemplated calling Daddy right now to come and get me out of this hellhole once and for all! When I went for my phone, Eric pushed me forward, my hands landing on my vanity. He was right on me with his hand around my neck from behind. He lightly squeezed as he tore off my robe. With his free hand, he unfastened his belt, unzipped his pants and took out his cock. "Eric . . . what-what are you doing?" He let his dick answer for him. He shoved inside of me, fast and hard. "Eric . . . uh, Eric." I moaned and cooed as he started bashing me from behind. The harder he fucked me, the tighter his grip was around my neck. Next, he snatched me up and threw me onto the bed. He stripped off the rest of his clothes and was all over me. When I had enough air in my lungs, I moaned for him to stop, but he didn't. He went harder. I got a little scared because he's never been this rough with me before. When he pint my legs back and started drilling my pussy, I whined, "Eric, please, you're hurting me. Stop!" As he started manhandling me, it became clear he wasn't going to stop. It was as if Eric had blacked out and turned into a different man. He was so rough and violent; I didn't recognize him. He was wrecking through my body so hard I started screaming, but that didn't stop him either.Once he finally finished inside of me, he kept his grip around my neck. His voice was low and rigid when he warned, "Now when I tell you I'm going to take a shower, you be a good wife and let me take a shower because next time . . . I-won't-stop." As he got off me, I didn't know what to say. Eric had just violated my body, and now he was threatening me. I was so scared and confused. I've never seen this side of my husband before—a side he threatened to bring back out the next time I stepped out of line. Well, I wasn't taking this from him. I'm out of here! "Eric, I'm leaving. I'm leaving, and I'm not coming back." My voice was rising quickly. "You don't get to hurt me! You don't get to take my body and abuse it. I'm not some dog chew toy; I am your wife!" He got up and went for his pants as if he didn't hear a word I just said. "Did you hear me, Eric? I'm leaving you. I'm done!" When he pulled out an envelope, he threw it over at me. My eyes burned through him when I asked, "What is that?" He swiftly answered, "Plane tickets. Jamaica, Katie. Just me and you. A whole week. No office. No cell phones. No nothing. We haven't officially taken a honeymoon yet because of my crazy schedule, but I'm taking some time now. I want to be with you, Katie, more than anything. And I'm . . ." He hesitated. "I'm sorry for what I did to you a second ago. I just got angry . . . and I'm tired . . . I-I just, baby, I'm sorry. Forgive me." I was a phone call away from filing a restraining order on Eric a second ago; now, here he comes with an apology and tickets to Jamaica? He's so unpredictable, which is what I love most about him. Suddenly, I didn't want to leave. I wanted to stay with my husband, and not because he's taking me to Jamaica. I'm staying because I love him, and I don't want to lose him. I was just frustrated before, that's all. He's home now, though. With me, and only me. He promised me there is not another woman on earth for him, and you know, I believe him. I'm the only woman for my husband, and I'm going to do everything in my power to keep it that way. When I rushed over to Eric, I wrapped my arms around him. "I love you so much." "I love you too, Katie. Just have faith in me, baby, and in us. I'm a good man that will never hurt you." As Eric and I started making out again, I believed him. I took every word he spoke to be true. "Come on, baby." Eric led me to the bathroom. "Let's go get nasty . . ."

Chapter Ten

COURTNEY

I sat at my desk staring at my computer screen, Erik heavy on my mind. He left early this morning for work without saying a whole lot to me. He kissed me and told me he'd be home later, that was it. I threw my ink pen down on my desk, wishing I could get some work done, but I can't. All I can do is think about my husband. I thought I was going to be okay with him being gone so much, but now it's really starting to take a toll on me. I realize he's a doctor with an insane traveling schedule, but this is just too much. I can't be in a marriage by myself, or with a man that's home for about seventy-two hours before he's gone again for days at a time. I'm starting to wonder what have I gotten myself into? Who did I really marry, and why is he never home? "Hi, Courtney." The voice that came toward me snapped me out of my trans. I took a deep sigh before I spoke to her. "Hey, Epiphany, how's it going." Epiphany Morgan is a teller here at the bank. She's kind of cute. If I liked girls, which I don't, I would probably give her a try. On second thought, I probably wouldn't. Mama would disown me if I brought a white girl home. She always said, "Son, if you can't use her comb, don't bring her home." So instead of a blonde hair, blue eyes, I got me a big black man! I don't think that's exactly what Mama had in mind. "Epiphany, what can I do for you?" "I need you to sign this for me, please. It's over my limit." It was a two-hundred-thousand-dollar cashier's check. I scribbled Courtney Byrd across the front and handed it back to her. Epiphany smiled at me and said, "Thank you." She caught me off guard when she asked, "Would you like to get something to eat after work? Maybe catch a movie or something?" Is she serious? I mean, I haven't come out and told the entire banking center staff and clientele that I'm gay, but I'm sure my sexuality isn't a secret. My waist is thinner than most of the girls that work here for heaven sakes! I keep my nails manicured; everything I wear is designer from my dry clean only cashmere knits, to my blended argyle socks. I wanted to scream, Epiphany, I'm married . . . to a man, you dumb bitch! but I didn't. Instead, I smiled back and said, "Can I take a rain check?" I don't think she was expecting that because she didn't say anything. She just looked at me as if I had crushed her dreams of having a romantic night out with me, which I did. "Uh . . . sure. Some other-some other time." I repeated, "Some other time." She turned around with a look of defeat. Maybe I should've just been honest: "Hey, Epiphany, hon, I'm gay, and married to a wonderful man, Dr. Erik Reynolds." I didn't want to do that to her and make her feel even worse. Besides, my personal business is just that: my-personal-business, which means it's none of hers or anyone else's at Citizens Bank. When my desk phone started to ring, I answered it with a dry, "This is Courtney." "Smile." The voice on the other end of the phone took me by surprise. It sounded like Erik, but I knew he'd be in meetings all day, so I didn't get my hopes up. I'm sure the caller was just another one of my old, creepy Monday morning customers calling in for me to balance his checkbook as if I studied at Yale for four years to balance a checkbook other than my own. "I miss you so much, baby." It wasn't some creepy customer; it's Erik! I perked up as a smile covered my lips. "Erik . . . This is a surprise." I got up to close the door to my office so that I wouldn't have any interruptions. "A good surprise, I trust. And why did you sound so down when you answered?" I didn't answer him because I started to cry right there on the phone. "Courtney, why are you crying?" "I-I miss you, Erik. I thought I could take you being away from me, but I can't." I sniffled. "I'm tired of waking up without you. I'm tired of going to bed alone. Eating dinner alone." "Court, please don't cry. I can hear you're upset, but I want you to calm down, babe. I'm right here." "No, you're not here, you're on the phone, Erik! You're never home. You're never with me. And when you are, it's not long before you're running out the door to leave again. I miss you." I cried harder. "I need you, Erik." "I know you do, Courtney, and I miss you too. I know these trips and seminar weekends are killing you, but they're killing me too." Were they really? I didn't hear any sobs coming from his end of the phone. I was the only one balling, doing that Oprah ugly cry thing again. "Look, I have a surprise for you." I'm listening. "When I get back from Boston this week, we're going to take a vacation." "A vacation?" I sniffled some more. "Yes, a vacation. I'm taking us to Jamaica." Whoa, Jamaica? I hope he wasn't talking about Jamaica, Queens. I am not going there. "Did you hear me, Courtney? We're going to Jamaica." I eased in with, "Jamaica, as in the island, right?" I know that was a dumb millennial question, but I have to be sure before I jump up and click the heels of my twelve-hundred-dollar Tanino Crisci's. "Yes, the island." He laughed. "Where did you think I was talking about, Queens?" "No . . . I just . . . This is just such a shock." My tears stopped instantly. "Does that mean you'll come with me?" I wanted to yell YES in twenty different languages. I'm sure the banking center could hear me screaming from behind my closed door because I was shouting at the top of my lungs. "Of course, I'll come with you!" I would follow this man anywhere. He knew that. Well, anywhere except for Jamaica, Queens. "Then it's set. I'll be home this Friday. We can leave Sunday. Just me and you. A whole week. No office. No interruptions. No cell phones. No nothing. We haven't officially taken our honeymoon yet because of my schedule, but I'm taking some time now, babe." My gloom quickly turned into something special with my husband on the other end of the phone, sounding as if he was reading a script from inside of my mind because he was saying exactly what I wanted to hear. It sucks that I have to spend the rest of the week without him, but come Friday morning, he was mine all mine, and I could not wait. "Hey Court, I have to jet, but I'll see you first thing Friday morning, okay. And stop all that crying; Daddy will make it all better Friday." I gripped my receiver when I said, "Friday morning, Daddy." Jamaica, here we come!

Chapter Eleven

KATIE

He held my hand on the plane. He held my hand in the lobby of the hotel as we patiently waited to be checked in. He even held my hand as we entered our hotel suite together. He's been holding my hand all day, and he's still holding my hand as we stroll seventeen thousand feet above the ground below at Lovers Leap in Jamaica. When I looked over at my husband and cracked an uneven smile, he grinned back at me and asked, "Katie, why are you looking at me like that?" I walked beside Eric admiring his perfectness. I guess I'm still in the honeymoon stage because I just can't seem to keep my eyes, or my hands, off him. Eric is a picture-perfect specimen from the top of his short black mane, to his oiled abs, all the way down to the bottom of his feet. I looked down at his manicured toes that were peeking through his Prada flip-flops. I quickly thought, I never knew Eric had a pair of Prada flip-flops. "What's on your mind, Katie?" He snapped me out of my sequestered thoughts of him. "Nothing in particular; just enjoying this beautiful scenery here with you." Eric smiled and looked down at the beige sand under our feet. "So, Eric, what's on your mind?" He answered, "My mind is always on you." He then nudged my shoulder. Before I could respond, he ran off into the short distance ahead of us. I questioned him as I giggle aloud. "Eric . . . What are you doing?" He didn't answer me. I call for him again. "Eric? . . ." He walked back over to me with a flower of some sort in his hand. I hope it's not poison ivy. "This is for you." I smiled when he handed it to me. "They call this flower Hibiscus. It's a genus flowering plant in the mallow family, Malvaceae." I looked up at him. "How did you know that?" He looked right into my eyes when he says, "I know a beautiful rarity when I see it." I wanted to melt right here in front of my husband from his soft words. "Why don't you put this right . . ." Eric took the flower from my fingertips and placed the stem behind my ear. "Here." He adjusted it a little. "It's perfect." He then kissed my lips ever so gently. I wasn't sure how long the kiss lasted because I was no longer present. I was swept away by Eric's romance. This must be what heaven feels like. He grabbed my hand, locked his fingers with mine, and restarted our walk. Our arms swung in-between us as the afternoon glow painted our bodies. "Eric, where do you see us in say . . . five years?" I don't know where that question came from. He surprised me when he said, "I don't think about the future . . . I live in the moment. We can't control the future no matter how hard we try, so why waste any time or energy trying? Planning for a future that we may never see is a setup for failure." Eric suddenly seemed distant, almost as if he was talking to himself. Not only talking to himself but in another world all by himself. "I live in the moment. I don't plan. I don't set aside. I don't save for a rainy day. I just live." He looked at me. "Everything happens for a reason." He looked away from me. "Everything happens just when and how it is supposed to happen." I asked, "Do you think we were supposed to just happen? Do you think we were meant to be?" He gave me the oddest look when he said, "Like I said, Katie . . . everything happens for a reason. You and I were meant to be together, so we're together. I chose you, so here we are." Did he choose me? What he should've said was I chose to let him have me, but I didn't want to mess up the mood with that small technicality. I rubbed his hairy arm when I said, "I love you, Eric." He looked at me as he speaks. "Katie, you mean the world to me. Regardless of what happens in our lives, I love you, and I thank you for becoming my wife." He lightly caressed the side of my face. "I gave you this flower because it reminds me of you: Beautiful and fair, alone in a patch full of thorns waiting to be rescued at just the right moment. Like that flower, I could've searched high and low to find you, but until the timing was right . . . until the stars lined up in the galaxy at the appropriate moment, you would've been next to impossible to find. But I did find you, and I'm grateful." Water started to roll down his cheeks. "Katie, I want to spend the time I have left on this earth, making you happy. All I can do is pray you'll allow me to. Accept me and all my flaws; have me as more than just your husband, baby. I want to be your best friend." He dropped down to his knees in front of me and latched onto the lower part of my body. I didn't know what to make of this. My husband was showing me yet another side of him. A side I had never seen before. He was so vulnerable, sensitive, and even defenseless at this moment. Who was this man latched onto my legs? Eric was usually so strong and in control, but not today. Today, he surrendered himself to me. Right here on the island, Eric and I shared a moment that I wished would last forever . . . Four Days Later . . . I sat silently in the backseat of the Uber that picked me up from the airport. The flight from Jamaica was exhausting. Or maybe I'm just exhausted. Besides all the sightseeing and shopping, Eric and I made love in every inch of our hotel suite. Eric and I made love in every inch of our hotel! In the steam room. In the shower off the beach. On the beach. In the lobby. I'm so glad we didn't get caught in the lobby. I watch enough Locked Up Abroad to know I would never want to be locked up abroad, especially if it meant being separated from my husband. No thank-you! But, of course, I am separated from him. As soon as our plane touched back down in Baltimore, he whisked me into an Uber right before he jumped into another one that headed in the opposite direction. The last thing I remember Eric saying to me was he had to take care of some business and promised he'd be home tonight. Maybe I'll make him a big dinner and prepare all his favorites. And then I'll serve his favorite dessert: Katie A La Carte. "Right here, driver!" If he kept his eyes on the road and out of the rearview mirror to look at my cleavage, he wouldn't have almost passed . . . my . . . What the . . . Whose truck is that in my driveway? I hopped out of the car the second the driver stopped. I didn't bother tipping him. Eric already took care of that, so I wasn't giving him another penny. When I got out of the smelly Mazda, I ran up the driveway. A brand-new black Range Rover was sitting there with a big red bow on top. I thought this must be a mistake as I searched in my bag for my cell phone to call Eric. Just as his name flashed across my screen with calling printed underneath, our front door swung open. It was Eric. He was inside the house. He made it here before I did, and in enough time to change clothes because he was wearing a totally different outfit from when I left him at the airport. Before I could walk up to him, he headed toward me. "You like?" "Eric, I don't understand. What is this?" "Just say you like it . . . It's yours." "Eric, what-what did you do? You didn't have to do this." "Katie, I know these past few months haven't been easy for you." I wanted to shout they sure haven't been. "This gift is just my way of saying thank you for sticking by me and not giving up on us." "Eric, I—" "Katie, I'm not finished." What came out of his mouth next was unexpected. "I want you to promise me, Katie. Promise me you'll never leave me." I froze. I didn't know what to say. I wasn't planning on leaving Eric. Well, there was that time I threatened to call my Daddy to come and rescue me, but I didn't make the call. I didn't leave my husband that night, and I'm not going to leave him now. I love Eric, and I love our life together. Sure, things can get a little rocky at times, but we get through it. "Forever, Katie." There he goes again. "Promise me we'll be together forever." Eric was scaring me. His eyes were scaring me. He looked at me almost the same as he did when we were in Jamaica at Lovers Leap right before he burst out into tears. "Please, Katie." He seemed to be shivering. And is he crying again? I didn't know what to say. I was at a complete loss, so I just threw my arms around him. I held my breath until he wrapped his strong arms around me. He is shivering. And yes, he is crying again. I eased back and looked up into his red eyes. "Eric, what is it?" "I don't want to lose you, Katie. I couldn't live without you." "Eric, you will never lose me." "Then promise me, Katie. Please, just promise me." "I-I promise, Eric. I promise I'll never leave you." There, I said it. I said what he wanted me to say right here outside for the world to see. Well, for our neighbors to see that is. I hope none of them are watching. Eric looked at me. His eyes widen. His face lit up with a smile. His tears seemed to be controlled because they were coming to an end. "What . . . what did you say, Katie?" "I said, I promise. I will never leave you. No matter what happens. No matter what we face, Eric, I will always be with you." I meant those words. I wouldn't leave Eric. I never actually planned on leaving no matter how many times I told myself I would. I love my husband with all my heart. "Thank you, Katie . . . You have just made me the happiest man on earth!" He picked me up and swung me around in his arms. We cried, laughed, hugged, and kissed all at once. We were together now forever. After all, I promised. I promised, and I meant it . . .

COURTNEY

Jamaica was so beautiful. I didn't want to come back to Baltimore. I tried to convince Erik to stay at least one more night; I think I even begged, but he wasn't having it, so here I am back in good old Maryland. Erik and I are back in the states, but I swear I left my brain in Jamaica because I can't keep my mind off our vacation. Oh Jamaica . . . The passion . . . The intensity. The fire that was ignited inside my husband was wild. He couldn't keep his hands off me, and I enjoyed every minute of it. I was praying we didn't get caught in the lobby. Now it's back to reality with me sitting in the back of some Uber all alone. As soon as our plane touched back down in the city, Erik threw me in a car with him heading to another one parked three cars away. I didn't want to see him go, and I told him so. He still left me, clamming he'd be home tonight. I didn't care about tonight; I wanted him with me now. The last thing I wanted was for him to be in a different car heading to God knows where to do God knows what.

He's supposed to be riding home with me. I perked up as the driver headed down my street. I couldn't wait to get home, grab my gym bag, a fresh white towel, and head straight to the gym. I need to work out some of the kinks my husband left behind. My body was so sore I could hardly move. Erik worked muscles on me I never even knew I had. I sat patiently as the driver inched to my destination. Once we stopped, I handed him a twenty-dollar bill and sent him on his way. Erik already paid for my ride, but I still decided to tip the guy. Erik said he took care of that too, but I wouldn't feel right getting out without giving the driver a little something for his troubles, better known as his J-O-B. When I got out of the car, I noticed a white Range Rover sitting in our driveway with a red bow on top. I don't remember buying a new SUV, and I'm sure my husband would've consulted with me before making an eighty-thousand-dollar purchase. By the time I made it back to the front of this beautiful piece of machinery, our front door swung open. It was Erik. I thought, what was he doing here? And when did he have time to change clothes? He trotted out to me. "You like?" "I . . . I . . . Erik, I love it, but—" "No buts, it's yours. I had it delivered this morning." I swallowed hard, trying to melt the golf ball sitting in my throat. "Court, I know these past six months haven't been easy for you." "Erik, you know we've—" He stopped me. "This gift is just a way for me to thank you for sticking by me and not giving up on us." Now, why did he think he had to reward me for not giving up on our marriage? When I said for better or worse, I meant it. Besides, we're good. "Promise me, Courtney . . ." His voice trailed off.

"Promise me you'll never leave me. No matter what, we'll always be together." Erik started to cry just as he had done in Jamaica right after he gave me this beautiful flower. He called it Hilbiscus, or Hibiscus . . . something like that. After he gave it to me, it was like he turned into someone else. I didn't even recognize him anymore. I'd never seen Erik cry before that day, and now, he was crying again, but why? "Courtney, please." "Erik, I would never leave you. The vows I made to you were forever and I—" "But I want to hear you say it now, Courtney . . . Just promise me." I looked right into my husband's eyes, and instantly I said, "I promise, Erik. I will never leave you," without any hesitation. After my promise filled the air, he held me close. Erik has never been shy about his sexuality or his display of public affection. He is a man, all man. There was no question about that. And he's in love with a man. There was no question about that either. He didn't care who seen us right there in the driveway making out like two teenagers on prom night, and neither did I. I hope our neighbors are watching. When he let me go, he looked at me. "Courtney, thank you. You have just made me the happiest man on earth!" Erik didn't have to thank me. I'm with him because I love him more than anything. Not because of some elaborate gift, and not because of the promise I just committed to. I'm with Erik and didn't plan on ever leaving him. That's a promise that would never be broken . . .

Chapter Thirteen

KATIE

As I try on another pair of Balenciaga heels, I've already made up in my mind that I'm going to charge them, along with every other pair of shoes I've tried on today. The women shopping around me all look to be purchasing one, maybe two pairs of shoes, but not me. I have Balenciaga, Gucci, Valentino, and some other high-priced stilettos and slingbacks littered at my feet, and I must have them all, even the ones that don't fit. In this case, size doesn't matter. Besides, they'll probably just get tossed to the back of my closet with everything else I have no intention of wearing, anyway. Once I slide my size six eight-inch Christian Louboutin's back on my feet, I head up to the register with the clerk following close behind me, carrying all my boxes of new shoes. Once she finished totaling me up, I wasn't surprised my Neiman's bill was well over three thousand dollars. No sweat. When I swipe my Black Card, with Mrs. Dr. Eric Reynolds on the front, I feel superior—like I'm better than any of these hags around me that appear to be shopping on a budget. I can always spot which shopper is broke just by watching. They'll pick up garments only to check the price tag first. Not me. When I'm shopping, I find the plushest seat in the store to wait for one of the personal shoppers to bring me a glass of their best champagne. Once I've seen enough, I swipe my Black Card and head for the glass doors with usually two associates trailing behind me carrying my packages out. Today was no different. The clerks hurried behind me, both with an armful of my purchases. I could offer to help, but I'm not carrying anything besides my crocodile Birkin bag that's swinging from my forearm. With the commission I just provided, you're damn right I want my packages brought out to my car. I'm leaving Neiman Marcus, not Walmart, so I expect nothing less than the royal treatment. Once the store help and I make it outside, I pull out my Chanel sunglasses to hide my eyes from the bright sun rays beaming down. Once the last bag is loaded onto my buttery soft camel leather seats, I don't bother thanking the help; I simply get in my Range Rover, wait for one of the associates to close my door, start the engine and glide away. I quickly pulled out of the parking spot and get comfortable as I make the trip back out to the suburbs. I had to get out of that store and fast. It's almost noon, right around the time the poor climbs out of bed, roll up their marijuana cigarettes to smoke, comb their kids' hair, and come to the mall knowing damn well rent money is supposed to be for rent, not Neiman's. I'm not dealing with that type of mall crowd today, so I'm hightailing it back out to Howard County where I belong. When I got close to home, I drive through my beautiful neighborhood, sipping my organic wheatgrass admiring the well-manicured backdrop of my life. The lawns are all freshly trimmed, and the waxed, glossy cars sitting in the driveways all look like mine: New and expensive. On my side of town, everything looks new and expensive because it is. The age-old saying goes God helps those who help themselves. Well, just looking through my neighborhood, I can tell God sure has helped each doctor, lawyer, and entertainer within a three-mile radius. When I pull up to my circular driveway, I ease out of my SUV with the cobblestones clapping under my heels. With at least five shopping bags in each hand, I head into my home. Once I'm in the foyer, I drop my packages and my purse. I slip out of my stilettos and head for the staircase. Once I make it up to the bathroom, I start to take out my long blonde extensions, my mink lashes, and all the makeup I hid under today. As I wipe the bronzer from my face, there is not a speckle of color left on my alabaster skin. I then strip out of my designer clothes, spanxs, and my sparkly diamonds. When I look at myself in the mirror, I don't resemble the woman who walked in. When I came into this house, my labels and red bottoms made me feel confident and special. My husband's money elevated my status, allowing me to look down on whomever I choose to. Now look at me; I'm lower than those bargain shoppers I made fun of earlier. I acted as if they were all beneath me because they didn't seem to have the lifestyle that I have. They couldn't compete because they weren't flashing money, lines of credit, and a rich doctor husband the way I was. I know it makes me look like a snobby bitch, but it's what validates me. I would never admit that to anyone, but it does. That's why I stay. I love my husband, and I made promises to him, but the only reason why I stay after he disappears for days at a time is because I'm Mrs. Doctor Eric Reynolds. That title is just as important as the labels I wear. I stay because of my beautiful home, British automobile, and luxury lifestyle. I can't leave my husband or the life he's afforded me behind, so here I am alone, strolling into our empty fifty-six hundred square foot bedroom. When I drape myself over our Swedish king size bed, I grab Eric's pajama shirt and allow my tears to soak my silk pillowcase. My thin body shakes as my sobbing fills the room. Those women at Neiman's, my sisters and everyone else that knows my life is probably envious of me, and for good cause. I have a perfect life, including a perfect husband that does everything for me, except come home. No woman should have to live this way. No wife should have to put up with a man she only sees fifty percent of the time. But I do. No matter how many times I think of leaving, I'm always here when he walks through that door, ready to suck his dick while getting prepared for his next exit. After I swallow down two sleeping pills with the swig of red wine left in the bottle beside the bed, I call Eric's cell. I knew he wouldn't answer, but just knowing I have a doctor-husband to call makes me rest ten times better than any sleeping pill ever could. When his voicemail picked up, all I could mutter was, "I love you, Eric," as the Ambien tablets sweep me away for the next twelve hours.

Chapter Fourteen

COURTNEY

"**H**ey, Courtney . . . where are you, babe?" I called out, "I'm in here," from the den while I worked on a huge presentation for work. It's already Wednesday, and this thing is due Friday morning. I knew with Erik being home, I wasn't going to get much accomplished, but I planned on doing my best. I need this promotion and that third-floor corner office that comes with it. When Erik came up behind me, I could hear his phone vibrating. He ignored it, and so did I. "Hey, baby." I quivered when he wrapped his arms around me. "I missed you so much." He kissed my neck when he was in reach. "I've missed you too, Erik." I reached up and kissed his awaiting lips. As he thumbed through a stack of mail, he asked, "What are you working on?" I put the pencil I was jotting notes with behind my ear. "I have a massive presentation due this Friday, and it has to be textbook perfect; my entire career is riding on it. If I nail this account, I could get a new office, and the big raise I deserve." When

Erik asked, "What about Fenmore's?" I looked over at him. "You know to open my own tapas bar is my dream, but when the time is right. I can't put my career and everything I've worked so hard for on hold until that happens, so I need this promotion." He paused for a half-second before he asked, "What if I said I could help you." "Erik, no. I-no, I don't want you involved." I shook my head when I said, "No," again. "I'm your husband, Court; anything you do, I would hope to be involved." "Erik, you know what I meant. I don't mix business and pleasure. That never ends well." "I can understand you feeling that way." My eyes landed down to my lap. "When the time and money are both right, I'm going to scout out a great location without going over budget; hire a good, solid, reliable staff, an accountant, attorney, interior designer, exterior designer . . ." I shrugged my shoulders as my dreams of owning my tapas bar fell to the floor. "It's a lot, but it'll happen when the time is right." "What if I told you the time was right now?" I opened my mouth to answer him, but when nothing came out, I turned back to my computer screen. I didn't want to talk about my derailed dreams anymore; I have work to finish. "I took care of all of it, Courtney." I ignored him. He's rambling something over there, but I'm not taking time to even respond. When he asked, "Did you hear me, Court?" I answered him back with an "mm-hmm," as I jotted figures down onto my notepad. "Courtney, you don't seem excited." I threw my pencil down on my desk and turned back toward him. "I'm not getting excited, Erik, because I have a lot of work to do. You asked me a hypothetical question. I answered it, so now I'm done." His eyebrows furred. "Baby, I didn't say what if I took care of it; I said I took care of it. It's all yours if you want it." My eyes followed as he popped his black leather briefcase opened. He pulled out papers and two sets of keys. I asked, "Erik, what-what are you doing? What's all that?" As he got up and headed over to me, he said, "I took care of location, staff, an accountant and a lawyer. I called in the best interior designers in Maryland, too. It's all yours, baby." I jumped up and hugged him tightly, my eyes filling with tears. "Erik, you didn't. You .. . no, you didn't." "I did, babe. I did it for you." I had to pinch myself to make sure Erik was really saying these words to me, and I wasn't just daydreaming like I do as he rambles on about Monday night football. This couldn't be happening, though. He found a location. An attorney . . . designers. This must be a dream, but I would've awakened by now. "I spoke with my investors this afternoon and drew this up." He pulled a lease from his briefcase for a property on Canterbury Road near The Ambassador. "We can go look at it now if you want." He jingled the keys. I can't believe it . . . The opportunity I've been waiting on since I graduated from college is now staring me right in the face. All I could do was sob tears of joy. "Courtney . . ." His voice was so gentle. "You know I hate it when you cry." His eyes became watery, looking into mine. "Did I do something wrong?" Absolutely not! He's doing everything right. I could never repay him for this, or express my gratitude for what he's done for me. "Erik . . . thank-thank you so much. You . . . I don't know why you did this, but thank you. Sometimes, I'm so hard on you because you're not always here when I want you to be . . . I know you're working, but the selfish part of me wants you home." I whimpered. "Please forgive me." I cried harder. "Forgive me for not being more understanding. Oh . . . Erik, I'm sorry. I'm sorry for being self-centered, thinking only of my needs while you're out working, providing for me like you did today." I couldn't speak any longer. No more words. Just light sniffles from my overjoyed heart. My husband has just made the impossible possible. If Shaun was here, he would say I was being dramatic, and I was, but I didn't care. I'm so happy, and I want the whole world to know it! "Would you like to go see the new building now, or would you whether go later?" "Let's go now! I can't wait to see it. I bet it'll be everything I've ever wanted." As I stood there, I started to pray. I didn't really know how to, but I felt as if I owed a few words to whoever was listening: Lord, thank You. Thank You for sending me such a great man and best friend. I don't know what I've done to deserve him, or any of what he does for me, but thank You . . . Erik grabbed me by the hand. "Let's go, Court. Let's go see Fenmore's." I walked beside my husband to the front door, beaming the whole way out, just thinking of how lucky I am.

Chapter Fifteen

KATIE

"What are you two doing here?" I looked at Kyle then down at Epiphany. They stood at my front door, looking as if they were waiting for the other to speak. "What is it? . . . Epiphany . . . What's going on?" I could tell from their faces something was wrong, but neither one of them said a word. They just stood there like tweedle dumb and tweedle dumber. "Katie, we need to talk to you." That was Kyle hiding behind a gigantic pair of COACH Sunglasses. I'm sure they're fake. When Epiphany asked, "Aren't you going to invite us in?" I didn't answer her. I turned my back and headed through the foyer, leaving them both standing there. I was hoping they wouldn't follow me, but of course, they did. I headed into the den with Kyle and Epiphany galloping behind me. I grabbed the Cosmo I'd been thumbing through all morning off the coffee table, plopped down on the sofa, and turned on the TV although it didn't stay on long enough for a clear picture to form on the large screen. Kyle put her sunglasses on her head when she said, "Katie, we need to talk now." Did this bitch really just turn off my television! I yelled, "Kyle, what the hell do you think you're doing?!" She looked at me before she threw a sealed manila envelope down on the coffee table. I looked at the envelope then back up into Kyle's hateful eyes. "What is that?" "I think you should open it." I couldn't stand to look at her for another second, so I focused my attention on my other sister. "Epiphany, what is this about?" "Katie . . ." She stalled. "Epiphany, what is it?" "It's about Eric." Now they both had my undivided attention. I scooted to the edge of the sofa as I suddenly felt ill—like I was going to lose my lunch. The room started to spin. Now it was doing cartwheels right along with my stomach. I wanted to know what was in that envelope, but I wouldn't dare look for myself. I was too afraid to. I didn't want to hear that something had happened to my husband. I couldn't take that. I wouldn't be able to survive behind it. "Katie?" When my eyes raked over to Epiphany, she said, "I" —She looked at Kyle, then back at me— "we have something to tell you." "Epiphany, what is this about?" "Why don't you open the envelope and see for yourself." That was Kyle. "Would one of you please just tell me what this is all—" Epiphany cut me off. "Katie . . . Katie, me and Kyle hired a private investigator." I jumped up from the loveseat and screeched, "You what?! Epiphany, repeat what you just said!" When she didn't answer fast enough, I glared at Kyle. "What in the hell is going on here?!" Kyle looked right into my eyes. "Katie, look, we're not here to start trouble, okay. We just . . . Eric, sweetie, something isn't right with him, and you know that. We all can see it." "We all can see what?! Somebody better tell me what is going on, and I mean RIGHT NOW!" Epiphany took over. She wrung her hands together when she said, "Since the wedding . . . even before the wedding, Katie, it's been a disconnect with Eric." I folded my arms across my chest, my silk kimono robe clinging to my shoulders. I almost laughed when I asked, "Is that what this is about? A disconnect? Eric has been nothing but kind and even loving to you both. I don't know what else either of you would be looking for from him." I swooped my hair behind my ear. "Epiphany, hon, if you or Kyle feel some sort of 'disconnect' with my husband, you two discuss that during allll of your free time because I don't want to hear it." Kyle raised her voice at least two octaves when she said, "The disconnect is not between Eric and us; it's between you and Eric, hon." She took a breath, put her hands on her fat hips, and came back with, "We're worried, Katie, and so is Mom and Dad. (We're, I thought to myself as I looked this bitch up and down as she continued to talk) We're worried for you because it seems like the longer you stay with Eric, the more bizarre things become." I started waving my hand in her face. "Whoa, whoa, whoa, where is all of this coming from? What is this? What are you and Mom and Dad so worried about from across town? How do any of you know what goes on between Erik and me?" Epiphany caught me off guard when she snapped, "Do you know what goes on between you and Eric? We may be 'across town,' but we see things. We see a lot, Katie, and we just want to make sure you're okay." I sat back down on the loveseat, staring out the patio doors to the pool. My tone was harsh when I asked, "Why are you two here? Why are you doing this?" I tried to hold in all the emotions that were erupting inside of me. I looked up at my sisters when I asked, "Why are Daddy and Mom so worried about me?" I hunched my shoulders, trying to throw them off, but I knew why. Eric and I don't exactly live as normal husband and wife, and apparently, everyone knows that no matter how hard I try to hide it. The fact that they saw through my perfect life façade feels just as bad as my life being anything but perfect. I smoothed my hair back with both hands before I asked them to leave. "Katie, we did this because we love you, and we want to make sure Eric isn't hiding anything from you." I didn't look at either of them when I said, "I want you both out of here, and I want you out now." "Katie, we only met with the PI twice. He found sealed records within the first twenty-four hours of us hiring him . . . sealed records on Eric, I don't think you know about." I stood back up. I had to jump in before this beast continued. "Kyle, did you hear me? I want you and Epiphany to leave! Eric will be home soon, and I want to make sure the house is spotless." "You know he's not coming home later." I screamed, "GET-OUT!" Epiphany reached over and snatched the envelope off the table. She ripped it open in search of the documents inside. "Katie, look . . . This is a sealed report of a diagnosis." I swallowed the lump in my throat, trying to clear my air passage before I passed out. I can't believe what I'm hearing. I thought, what is she saying? What diagnosis? "Epiphany, please . . . Put those papers away and leave my house." She didn't listen to me. She kept reading. "He was diagnosed with schizophrenia and personality disorder when he was twelve. He was prescribed a treatment med called Antipsychotic back in two thousand." What the hell was she saying to me? My husband is a doctor. He doesn't have schizophrenia. If Eric did have any medical conditions, I would be the first to know, right? I'm his wife . . . he tells me everything. When I picked up my phone and started dialing, Kyle asked, "Katie, who are you calling?" "The police department. I asked you two to leave, but you're still here. Now you're trespassing." "Katie, would you just listen to what she has to say?" Epiphany looked over at Kyle before her eyes were back in my direction. "Let's just go, Kyle. Let's give her some time to cool off." "Take it all with you . . . all those papers and lies; take your envelope full of bullshit out of here!" Epiphany mouthed, "I'm sorry, Katie," before she followed Kyle's wide back to the front door. When Kyle turned around and said, "Please call us if you need us," I fanned my hand at her and said, "Screw you, bitch." The artwork on the walls vibrated when I slammed the door. I rushed back to the den and grabbed my phone. I didn't take a minute to process any of what I just heard. All I want is for Eric to tell me it's not true. That's it. I can't feel anything or take my next breath until he does. My hands trembled as I dialed Eric's number. Each ring in my ear felt like daggers making their way through my skull. "Katie? . . ." "Eric!" "Katie, can you hear me?" Through the static, I yelled out, "Eric! Eric, where are you?!" "Katie . . . Can you hear me?"

Chapter Sixteen

COURTNEY

"Knock, Knock." It was Erik standing at my office door. "Hey, come on in. You're right on time, Dr. Reynolds." Erik came to the bank to finalize contracts for Fenmore's. Soon my tapas bar will be opened for business. My place was going to be the newest and hottest hotspot in Baltimore, but not before these new contracts were signed, notarized, sealed, and delivered. Erik sat down in front of my desk and crossed his legs. Well, his right ankle landed on top of his left kneecap. I'm not sure if that qualifies as a leg cross, but he looked sexy doing it. "Courtney, how about we grab some lunch after we're finished here? We can head to Ceriello's over on Belvedere. I've been craving Italian all week." "Oh, yes, that sounds good. I'll send my assistant an air message and have her make our reservations. We can head over as soon as we're finished here." Before I could get my words out, my eyes landed on the front door of the crowded banking center. It was one of the tellers storming back in from another one of her overly long lunch breaks with what looked like tears in her eyes, obviously upset about something. "I swear white women can be so dramatic." I cracked a smile at my stereotypically driven comment. Erik looked at the teller running through the lobby then quickly back at me. "What's her deal?" he asked calmly. "That's Epiphany Morgan; she works here." I took my eyes off the teller station where Epiphany now stood and looked at him. My attention was now focused on trying to figure out a way to get my husband butt-naked and on top of my desk without anyone noticing. I looked at him. He looked at me. He then looked down at the front of his body as if I had just detected a noticeable wrinkle in his wardrobe. "Courtney, why are you looking at me like that?" "Are you thinking what I'm thinking?" He looked around, then back at me. I could tell by the devilish grin on his lips he was thinking exactly what I was thinking. "Courtney, we can't . . . Not here. Not now." "Why not? I have blinds, and both doors close and lock." I looked over at the door behind me, leading to the employee side of the bank, then over at the main door leading out to the lobby. He laughed me off. "Courtney, we can't, baby." Before my next entreat for my husband to screw me on top of my desk until I sang the Star-Spangled Banner backward, Epiphany was heading toward my office. She had perfect timing because I was ready for her to meet the real reason why I turned down all her invites to lunch, to the movies, dinner, and even her friend requests on Facebook. I'm a married man, happily married to a happily married man. It sounds more confusing than it really is. I'll let her down easy with something like Hey girl; I'm gay! I giggled as I got up to meet her in the lobby. I wanted to break the news to her first before she met Erik. "Erik, I'll be right back." I walked past him and met Epiphany inches away from my office. She was holding a commercial loan app she needed preapproved. When she stopped in front of me, I could see tears resting in her eyes. "Epiphany, what's wrong?" I didn't want to date her, but I considered her somewhat of a friend, and I was genuinely concerned. "It's nothing." I could tell more was coming, and I was right. "Me and my sisters just got into a huge fight." She broke down right in front of the entire banking center and me. God, I wish I hadn't asked what was wrong with her. I guess I wasn't that concerned, after all. "Why don't you come into my office for a second and collect yourself. I'll take care of the preapproval, and then maybe you can join us for lunch." Her watery green eyes looked into mine. "Us?" "Yes, I want you to meet someone." Just because she was all broke up over some catfight she had with her sisters on her lunch break did not mean she wasn't going to meet my husband. I'm getting this out in the open right here, right now. By the time I made it back to my office, Erik was gone. In the sixty-five seconds I spent with Epiphany right outside my doorway, my husband had vanished. "Epiphany have a seat . . . Give me one second." She sat down where Erik had been sitting. I poked my head back out into the lobby, but he wasn't out there. "Courtney, who are you looking for?" I ignored Epiphany. I headed out the second door to my office in route to find Erik. I couldn't imagine he'd be in the back wing of the bank since it was only for employees. The second I made it out into the hallway, I spotted him heading for the exit with his phone up to his ear. I raced behind him, but I didn't catch him before he made it out the glass door marked Employee's Only. When I made it outside, I shouted, "Erik!" He didn't respond. I got closer to him. "Erik, where are you going?" No answer. He tended to his phone call, almost as if I wasn't running behind him. "Erik, wait!" When I got in-ears reach, I heard him saying, "Katie? . . . Katie, can you hear me?" He then ended the phone call and stuffed his cell deep into his pocket. When he finally turned to me, I asked, "Why did you leave? We aren't finished with the contracts," but he didn't answer me. "And who is Katie and why were you shouting at her? . . ." Before I could finish questioning him, Erik grabbed me. He snatched me up and forced me toward his car that was only steps away from us. "Erik, what are you doing? Where are you taking me? I'm still working!" He unlocked the doors to his Beamer and literally threw me inside. It took me a moment to realize what was happening, so I sat on the plush leather frozen. I watched Erik through the windshield race around to the other side of the car. He jumped in, started the engine, and sped off. I screamed, "What are you doing?!" without an answer from him. Instead, he jetted to the freeway dodging every other car in sight. I looked over at him with terror in my face. "Erik, what are you . . ." Oh no! We almost crashed into the back of an ambulance. "Erik, stop! . . . Slow down!" Erik didn't show any signs of emotions as he drove. He whipped the car with his arms extended to the steering wheel like he was handling a racing game at an arcade. I shouted, "Erik, would you please slow down!" He didn't. He drove like a madman until we reached our home. He turned my familiar, pleasant, thirty-minute car ride into twelve and a half minutes of reckless horror. He turned into our driveway, slammed his BMW in park, hopped out and decided I was coming with him . . . from his side of the car. He grabbed hold of my suit jacket and dragged me out of my seat, over his seat, and out to the pavement. "Erik, what . . . what are . . ." We were tussling right outside in the driveway. "What are you doing? Would you stop this!" He opened the garage and forced me inside. As I'm heading into the house, I could hear the right garage door closing. Once I got into the kitchen, I turned back toward the door I left open to wait for my husband to come in the house, but he was already standing right in front of me. His eyes read anger; his body language told me to beware, but why? What had I done to make him so upset? I didn't have time to ask because now his hands were wrapped around my neck. I gasped for air. I couldn't breathe as he chocked me. What the hell was going on here?! I coughed. I swatted at his hands, but it was no use. He wasn't letting up. I fought him, but he was getting the best out of me. When he reached for my neck again, I thought about scooping up one of the knives in the knife block only a few reaches away to defend myself, but I couldn't reach it. "Erik!" Cough, cough,

cough. "Erik, . . . what are you doing?" Oh, shit! I think my whole life just flashed in front of my eyes. I feel weak . . . unable to fight as hard as I was a minute ago. My thoughts we're becoming far and in between as I counted the seconds in the air. I could no longer speak, gasp, cough, or breathe. Erik was right in front of me, but I could barely make out who he was. My eyes were wide open, but the room was starting to go black. I could feel Erik's breath on my face, but I couldn't see him. I was no longer fighting for my life because I couldn't move anymore. All the torture inside of my husband's hands was over. I couldn't feel anything . . . My mind was still running, but my lifeless body had plummeted to the floor a few seconds ago. I lied in darkness. Total black, cold, eerie darkness. I had lost all consciousness by the time Erik picked me up off the floor and carried me toward the staircase, with my last thought being what the hell just happened? . . . One Hour Later . . . I awakened slowly, rubbing my temples as my eyes gradually opened a little wider. I blinked a few quick times to get the room into focus without any luck. Everything was still hazy. I even had a hard time making out the numbers that were reading across the digital clock on the nightstand next to the bed. I sat up and stretched with a big yawn quickly to follow. When my eyes reopened, I noticed him sitting there. I almost jumped out of my skin. Screw almost, I jumped out of my skin. My abuser was only inches away from me, looking as if he was ready for round two. He apparently had been watching me as I slept. Maybe he was waiting for me to wake up so he could finish the job.

"You're awake." I just looked at him and didn't say a word. "Do you need anything? Do you want some tea? Let me get you some water." When Erik got up, I stopped him with, "I don't want any water or tea." He asked, "Okay . . . Well, what do you want, baby?" I sat up straight when I said, "All I want to know is, who is Katie?" All the color suddenly flushed from Erik's face. He turned as pale as our bedroom walls once I quizzed him. He was shouting her name earlier, so I want to know who this chick is, so I asked him again, "Erik, who is Katie? I heard you on the phone with her earlier." I rubbed my neck. "I heard you loud and clear." He handed me a bottle of DASANI. I put it on the table without opening it. "Erik, who in the hell is Katie?!" "She's the lead hygienist at my practice. She called me earlier to let me know about a troublesome patient. I got up from your desk when she called to get a little privacy, but when I got outside, we lost signal. I couldn't hear her anymore. That's when you ran up." "Yeah, and that's when you chocked me out." Erik looked away from me as if he couldn't stand to look into my eyes any longer. "I lost my temper earlier, Court; I should never have done that to you, though. I shouldn't have put my hands on you. I just-baby, I blacked out. I lost it after the hygienist called. It's a lot going on in my office, but . . . look, babe, there is no excuse for what I did earlier. I'm so sorry." Looking at him right now makes me want to hate him. And I don't give a damn about that phone call, or some troublesome patient. He had no right to do this to me. No fuckin' right! I snapped, "I want to meet her!" "Who-what?"

"Katie . . . She's your head hygienist, so I feel like I should have met her by now, right? Her, or at least someone from your staff." Erik has a private practice in Great Falls, about an hour away. I've been there before, but I don't remember seeing a Katie. Actually, I don't remember seeing anyone at all. We strolled through the well-equipped office several times, but always after hours. "Did you hear me, Erik?" "Yeah, but, Court, I can't do that. She's-she is not on site right now." I jumped up. "Make it happen. I want to meet this woman." "Courtney, why are you doing this? It was work earlier, babe. Just-work." I stood up. "'Just work,' don't leave me bruised." Before he responded, I headed for the bathroom. I said, "I want to meet her, Erik, and that's final!" before I slammed the door behind me.

Chapter Seventeen

KATIE

Two Months Later . . . I lie out under the warm September sun listening to the splash of water as my husband does laps from one end of the pool to the other. I peek out from behind my shaded lenses to watch his long, strong arms come up out of the crystal-clear water, and gently glide back in. His frame moved like a trained dolphin as he controlled the motions of his lean physique. On his fifth lap back from the deep end, his wet body stood stagnated in the water as he looked up at me lying there in my white two-piece bikini. "Katie, you look so damn sexy up there. How about I come to join you." Since the blowout with my sisters a few months ago, I haven't spoken to either of them or our parents. Their invasion was the last straw for me. If something were going on with my husband, I wouldn't need some cheap, bogus private investigator to tell me so. I haven't mentioned the fight to Eric, and I wasn't going to. He'll just try and find the good in what they did, giving their fat asses a pass, and let it go. That's not how I planned on handling the situation, so I kept it to myself. As Eric gets out of the pool and head to the chair beside me, I don't see schizo or anything close to it. Honey, all I see is an overworked doctor, with a beautiful blonde for a wife. When he got comfortable beside me, he said, "Katie, I was thinking, how about we go out tonight?" "Sounds good . . . where did you have in mind?" He casually answered, "Fenmore's." "You know, I think I saw an ad for that place on Facebook or something. Isn't that the new restaurant over on Canterbury Road?" "That's it. It just opened this past Saturday. My receptionist was raving about it when she came into the office on Monday, so I thought we could go and check it out." "How about we do that, Dr. Reynolds." "Okay, baby. We'll have fun, maybe go to a club afterward." Eric got up. "Babe, I'm going to go wash off before I head to the office." He kneeled and kissed me. "I'll be back to pick you up around eight o'clock." He kissed me again before he headed into the house through the piazza. No sooner than Eric left, my phone rang. To my surprise, it was Epiphany. I was about to ignore her, but I went ahead and answered it. "Hello." "Hey." "Hey." "I wanted to check on you, Katie; we haven't talked in a few weeks." "Epiphany, honestly, I don't want to go back to a few weeks ago." I took a deep breath. I didn't want to fight, at least not with Epiphany. "Just be my little sister, okay . . . I appreciate you looking out and trying to protect me but know everything is fine between Eric and me. My husband isn't sick. He isn't distant or disconnected from me or our marriage. Trust me, we're fine. Now, can we please just move on? I can't fight with you or your other sister anymore." "Deal." Damn, that was fast. She didn't fight me or bring up that stupid PI, thank God. "So, what are you up to? Let's go to the mall. Eric and I have a date tonight, and I don't have a thing to wear." Epiphany laughed. "You probably have more clothes than me and Kyle combined." Now I was laughing too because she was probably right. "Where are you guys going?" "Eric wants to go to that new spot over on Canterbury Road." "The Ambassador?" "No, it's a new place. I think it's called Fennmore's or something like that." "Oh, I know that place. The owner, Courtney, used to work at Citizens." When she asked, "You guys mind if I tag along?" I so wanted to tell her hell no, but I guess she can come. "I haven't seen Courtney since he resigned from the bank a few months ago, so it'll be nice to see him." "Okay, well, come with. I'm sure Eric won't mind. I'll come by and pick you up in about an hour, so we can hit up a few boutiques before we head out to Eastpointe." Epiphany's tone was cheery, as was mine. "Okay, I'll be ready. We are going to have so much fun tonight, sis . . ."

Chapter Eighteen

COURTNEY

Here I am spending another evening running around Fenmore's like a chicken with his head blown off. I swear, since I left Citizens, I haven't slept a wink. I guess I didn't realize being a business owner would be this much work, but I'm here for it. Along with overseeing every aspect of my new place, each morning, I have to make sure the menu selection for that particular day is just right. The wine colonnade must be fully stocked with only the finest assortments. Then there's the staff. I try my best to keep them as comfortable as possible, or at least satisfied during their shifts so they won't haul off and kill each other, or worse, haul off and kill me! So far, I'm still breathing, so I must be doing something right. I feel like I owe Erik my life for helping me fulfill my dream. I always knew Fenmore's would happen, but never in my wildest imagination did I think it would happen so fast, so big, or so elegant. My joint was ornamented with everything from marble countertops in the luxurious lavatories to stainless steel service equipment in the fifteen thousand square foot kitchen. I won't even mention the live waterfall that flows under the glass lounge area furnished with Italian imported leather. It's been almost a week, and I still can't believe it's my tapas bar. Erik made this possible for me, and I couldn't be happier. "Byrd, I need you to approve the seating chart for that big book signing party next Friday." That was Shaun. I recruited him as my official events planner. I wanted Fenmore's to be known for the most fabulous parties this side of the Potomac River, so what did I do? I employ Mr. Fabulous himself, Shaun Price. Now, if I can just get him to stop calling me Byrd, I'll be even happier. "Nick Haskins will be in Baltimore next Friday. He wants to have his release party here for his new book, Betrayed." I needed Shaun to handle this release party business . . . on-his-own. That means the seating chart, the menu, the music selection, and anything else that comes along with this book release party because I just don't have time. I have other, more important business to take care of like running the place. "What's up, Shaun?" I turned around the second I heard my husband's voice. He spoke to Shaun but quickly headed over to me. I wanted to kiss him, but he beat me to it. Erik reached down and planted a nice wet one right on the center of my puckered lips. When our kiss ended, he looked into my eyes. "Hi, Courtney." "Well, hello yourself, Erik." I licked my lips right before I said, "This is certainly a surprise. What are you doing here so early?" "I had a little time in-between patients, so here I am. I wanted to see you." "I'm glad you came." We sat at the empty bar with Shaun and the rest of the staff taking over my position as the headless chicken. "How does it feel to be in business a full five days?" Technically, I've been in business for six days, but Fenmore's is closed on Sundays. Mama always said, 'Sunday is the Lord's Day.' And I planned on giving that exact explanation to my mama if she ever asked why I decided to close on Sundays. Truth be told, Sunday is my day to rest. I'm not running to some mega-church with ten percent of my earnings to furnish some long-winded pastor another luxury. No thanks, so skip the Lord's Day; Sunday is Courtney's day. Hallelujah! "Everything is running smoothly. There are a few bumps here and there, but I'm managing." Erik looked over at Shaun. "How is he working out?" "He's great. Other than irritating me with every single detail of the events he is supposed to be planning, he's good." "Well, if you need any help with anything, you know I'm here for you. You're not in this alone." "Yeah, yeah, yeah, you're just protecting your investment." I seriously joked. Erik smiled. "You know that's not what I'm doing. I just want to make sure you're happy Court, that's all." "Well, I am happy, thanks to you." Erik got up from the stool. "I have to get going. I have an appointment in thirty minutes. I'll be back tonight. I have a surprise for you." He knows I hate surprises. "I have someone I want you to meet. She's very special to me." I hope it isn't that damn Aunt Ollie from Toledo he's always talking about. "I have to run." He kissed me. "I'll see you in a few hours." "Okay. Call me if you get a free moment." He winked at me and said, "I will" before heading for the door. "Where is that fine-ass husband of yours running off to now?" That was Shaun. "He has a patient coming in soon, so he had to jet." As I started flipping through my phone for the poultry vendor's phone number, I said, "Shaun, I'm going to need you to man the place tonight. Erik will be here, and he says there is someone he wants me to meet." Shaun quickly asked, "Who is it?" "I don't know." I kept my answers short. "Courtney, . . . do you ever find Erik . . . You know I love Erik, so please don't think I'm trying to be shady, but do you ever find his behavior a little strange?" I looked at Shaun and asked, "Strange?" "Yeah, like Erik and his family, or lack thereof. He never brings any of them around; at least I've never met any of his family. He's obviously not shy about you or his feelings for you, yet he seems to keep you hidden." Right then, I went from zero to sixty! I was about ready to pop from the anger I felt creeping down my spine. "Shaun, what is that supposed to mean?" "It means . . ." He hesitated as if he was trying to choose his words lightly. And he should be. Hell, he better be! But he didn't. "Courtney, why is it always just Erik? I never see any family, close friends, or any of his—" I cut him off. "Shaun, his parents were killed years ago. I already told you that." "Okay, soooooo he doesn't have any brothers or sisters?" "No." "No cousins, uncles, aunts?" Well, there is Aunt Ollie . . . I glared at Shaun. "Shaun, what are you implying?" He looked down then back up at me. "Courtney, you know how much I love and respect Erik, and I think he is a really good choice for you." I jumped in with, "A damn good choice!" "Okay, and that's a good thing, but I'm still questioning him, and wondering why is it always only him. I've never seen any extensions of him. His parents were killed, but what about the rest of his family? There is not even a distant cousin in the picture? No friends? No nobody? Nothing but him, his briefcase, and his weekly goodbyes." I snapped my head over to Shaun after I threw my phone down on the bar. "Shaun, where is all this coming from?" "Girl, I'm sorry if it sounds like I'm coming for Erik, but—" "But that's exactly what you're not going to do, though!" My face muscles were tight and frowned. "Bitch, I'm not about to stand here and let you question my husband or research his family tree." "I bet you're not because I'm sure you don't know yourself." When I gasped, Shaun came back with, "Courtney, you already know imma keep it real with you, girl. I've held this in long enough." "You've held what in long…" I stopped myself. I wasn't about to go back and forth with Shaun, especially when it came to Erik. I been done snapped out on him before I could catch myself, so let me defuse this real quick before it gets out of control real quick. "Now look, Miss Thing, I love my husband, he loves me, and that's all that matters. Let's move on before you piss me off in here and make me cause a scene. Since it's my name on the lease, that would not be a good look. Now I'm going to need you to tighten up, get to work, and stop gossiping about the boss and his husband." I thought, you stupid motherfucker! Who the hell does he think he is asking those types of questions about Erik? I pay him to plan events, not pry into my husband's personal life! "I'm sorry, Byrd. I really am. I wasn't trying to make you mad or mess with your concentration, knowing you have so much to do." I didn't want Shaun to apologize; I just want him to be smarter and stay out of my married business.

Besides, I already have enough doubts and questions that swarm my head daily when it comes to my husband, so I don't need Shaun adding any more uncertainties. In my marriage, what others see as uncommon was normalcy for me. Or maybe it was just love that blocks me from seeing Erik how everybody else probably sees him. I grabbed my keys from behind the bar to head out. "Shaun, call me if you guys need anything. I'll text and check in soon." I hightailed it out of there. I didn't have time for Shaun; I have to get ready for tonight. Erik said he has someone very special he wants me to meet. I just wonder who she is . . .

Chapter Nineteen

KATIE

I shiver as I sit alone in this new space I now know as Fenmore's. Eric told me he would pick me up at eight o'clock sharp, but he never showed. Instead, he sent a car for me. I rode here by myself. I walked in by myself. And now, I'm sitting all by myself. It's not the chilly temperature breezing through the room that bothers me; I shudder as I ponder what could have my husband so occupied that he not only skipped picking me up like he promised he would but also has him so busy that he can't answer any of my calls. Where could he be? Epiphany is also running late, but she did text to let me know she's on her way. If she weren't coming, I would get up and leave. I just want to go home at this point. No one would miss me anyway. No one would even care that I was gone. Not even my husband. I was all set for a night of expensive wine, soft music, spoken complements, and my husband right by my side. As I sit here alone, I stare out to the gallery imagining Eric whisking me out there where he would kiss me under the stars with us becoming one with the soft, bright moonlight. Ugh, why the hell did he invite me to some cheesy tapas bar only to be a no show? I want out of this place so I can just go home. "Hey, Katie." When I turned toward the staircase, Epiphany was coming up. When she made it up to the lounge, we hugged. She said, "You look so pretty." I wanted to say, Of course, I do, sweetie. "You're a cutie tonight, too, hon." That's defiantly not what I wanted to say looking at her cheap outfit. "I'm sorry I'm so late getting up here. I stopped downstairs and visited with my friend from the bank. Remember, I told you we worked together at Citizens. I'm so proud of him." I thought I don't care, Epiphany! "Hey, where is Eric?" "Eric, he . . . uh. He didn't . . . He's running . . ." "Hello, ladies." Just as I was trying to explain another one of Eric's absences, he walked up to us. He was wearing a cream suit, black dress shirt, and black loafers. I could tell his hair had been freshly cut; his goatee was perfectly trimmed, and his fingernails had a slight gloss to them. I swear he looked like he just stepped out of an editorial of some high fashion Italian magazine. He looks so good standing there, I'm seconds away from forgetting he's almost two hours late. "Good evening, Epiphany. It's always good to see you." He gave her a hug and a kiss. "Where is Kyle?" I jumped in with, "She had to work." Eric's dark, sexy eyes were now on me. After he kissed me on the cheek, he said, "Katie, you look beautiful." I blushed. "Thank you. You're not looking too bad yourself." After a few minutes of us chatting, Eric said, "Katie, there is someone I want you to meet." He then turned around with a quick gesture to follow. Seconds later, someone was coming up the small staircase. He turned back to me once his guest was in route up to us. "Who is it, Eric?" Eric instantly introduced us. "Katie, this is Courtney." My arm reached for the extended hand, waiting for me. "Courtney, this is my lovely wife, Katie." I smiled as we shook hands. My tone was friendly when I said, "Hello, Courtney . . . it's so nice to meet you . . ."

Chapter Twenty

COURTNEY

Goddamnit! I cannot believe this. Tonight, of all nights, not one, but all three of my hostesses called off, leaving me to fend for myself. They oversee pretty much everything for the patrons, but they're not here! What the hell am I going to do? Fenmore's was the kind of experience where it wasn't uncommon for the entrees to be served by the chef himself. Sometimes, still ablaze, the culinary expert would hand-deliver each selection to its designated area, but not tonight. We're much too busy for such service, so that's where my hostesses would have come into place. But since there isn't one in the entire building, I guess that's where I come into place. I could easily finesse my way through tonight if Erik weren't coming later. God, I didn't want to be drenched in sweat and smelling like food when he gets here. And he wants me to meet someone? I don't think I can do that now. I'm all tensed, and I'm sure my frown lines are etched into my moist skin. Erik's friend, or whoever it is, is going to

109

hate me. She'll hate me and question Erik as to why he chose me. She'll probably think I'm just some greasy fry cook from the hood that got my start down at the local McDonalds. After all, sweat, cologne, and olive oil didn't precisely scream Ivy League education! Well, I am wearing Armani if that counted for anything. It doesn't! She'll probably think my suit is a knock-off after labeling me a fraud. She'll think I'm nothing more than some guy fulfilling Erik's gay phase. She won't see me as he sees me. I wanted to shout, Erik loves me, and I love him, lady! Why can't she see that! I quickly take a sip from the glass in my hand. I was on my way to the center area of Fenmore's to deliver this aging house special, but I didn't quite make it. I'll have to pour another glass because I almost downed this one in one gulp. I just needed something to calm me down—something to release the fear that drove me into full-blown panic. Why would I assume Erik's guest would think any of those things about me? I'm sure my husband gave her a complete rundown on me and my bio. Furthermore, who is this person anyway? Erik never told me exactly who I was meeting tonight. All he said was he had someone very special he wanted me to meet. Maybe if he would answer his phone, or at least return a text, I could get to more answers. I licked my wet lips as I stir the rest of the wine in the glass. Chateau Lafite 1787 did the trick. I felt calm now, relaxed even. I suddenly no longer cared who Erik was bringing here tonight or what her perception of me would be. NOT! I'm still a nervous wreck, and this six-figure liquor isn't helping at all. If anything, it's just making me tipsy. Erik's visitor won't only look at me as a knock-off wearing fry cook from

McDonald's, but also a drunk. I laughed to myself as my thoughts seemed not so serious anymore. Don't get me wrong, I'm still freaking out, but it suddenly felt funny now. Make that hilarious! I thought, no wonder Erik never lets me drink. Well, Erik isn't here yet, so bottoms up. "Excuse me, Courtney." One of my employees snapped me out of what felt like a drunken stupor the second time she called my name. I turned to the help as my eyes seemed to be hanging lower and lower, and lower. I tried to straighten my posture as best as I could, but it was no use. I'm plastered, and I'm sure it showed. I tightened my tie thinking, it's all good. What was my employee going to do? Fire me? I own the place, bitch! I hissed when, "Yes, Victoria," shot out of my mouth. Couldn't she tell I didn't want to be disturbed! "Someone is here to see you." Now I should fire her. Who the hell is this someone? "Is it Epiphany Morgan again? Can you please tell her I'm busy, and we'll chat later?" "No, it isn't her." I'm sure my sarcastic tone made her feel really silly when I smiled and said, "Victoria, hon, do you know who's waiting for me?" Before she could answer, I took off, passed her. If I would've looked into her stupid-ass face another minute, I probably would've coughed up my dinner. I laid the empty glass down and headed out into the main area. "Hey, Courtney." It was Shaun standing there signing a clipboard for a delivery. "Victoria didn't have to bother you; I'll take care of this." "Good, because I'm about to steal Courtney away for a little while." It was Erick. He walked up behind Shaun, and the delivery guy, heading toward me. "Hey, Erik." I smiled as I took a few steps toward him to wrap my arms around him. He quickly released me and looked down into my eyes. "Courtney, are you okay? Your eyes are a little glassy." "I'm fine. I'm-I'm good." "Are you sure?" "I'm fine, Erik." I smiled brighter. "I just had a few glasses of very expensive wine is all." "You're nervous about tonight, aren't you?" "A little . . . make that a lot." I couldn't lie. "Well, I want you to relax. You have nothing to be nervous about." Before I knew it, Erik and I were heading to the staircase for the second-story lounge. "Come with me." When he said, "Wait right here, babe," I stopped at the bottom of the staircase as he headed up. Before long, Erik turned to me and signaled for me to come up to where he was. I took a deep breath, straightened my suit jacket and posture, and headed up. Erik wasted no time. As soon as our eyes met, he introduced us. "Courtney, this is Katie." I thought, oh, so this is Katie as I reached my hand out to her with a big, bright smile on my face. "Katie, this is my wife, Courtney." She looked at me for a second, almost as if she was sizing me up. Maybe she was because I was for damn sure sizing her up. I wanted to know who she was and why Erik considered her so special. I've heard her name leave his mouth before, but he's never offered any explanations about Katie other than she was a hygienist at his practice. As Erik's introductions continued, I was hoping I would learn a lot more tonight about Katie.

Chapter Twenty-One

KATIE

I shook Courtney's hand, probably longer than I should have. When I finally let go, her chunky fingers fell back down to her sides. She was kind of scruffy and fat, pushing at least three hundred plus pounds. And her dirty strawberry blonde hair looked to be littered with gray strands. This Courtney was a sight to see. She even made Epiphany look good sitting there. When Eric said he had someone he wanted me to meet, she's not who I was expecting. I never pictured my husband associating with someone like Courtney. Her skin was all oily, accompanied by noticeable breakouts and a few dozen blackheads. Her breasts looked to be soon making one with her stomach; she wore wire-framed glasses, she smelled funny, and her voice might've been an octave deeper than Eric's. "Katie, Courtney has been my head hygienist for many years." That was Eric's voice shooting out toward me. "She's very beneficial to me and my practice. She's like my right hand." 'Very beneficial?' 'My right hand?' I thought, since when? I've never even heard him mention a head hygienist before. From Eric's strange behavior alone, if Courtney looked even halfway decent, I would be a little concerned right now and would have Eric's right hand chopped off. He's left-handed anyway. Something tells me I have nothing to be worried about, though. If I weren't so trimmed and beautiful, with straight white teeth and thin ankles, Eric still wouldn't touch Courtney. Ew, at least I hope he wouldn't. "Epiphany, . . . Katie, there is someone else I want you two to meet." When Eric motioned again, a tall, stout gentleman walked up to us with a little girl by his side. "Katie, this is my brother Thaddeus Reynolds, we all call him Thad for short." Eric looked down at the little girl. "And this is his daughter, my adorable niece, Miranda." So now I'm really confused. Why is Eric introducing all of us now? One would think he would've taken care of these formalities before we got married, or at least at the reception. "It's nice to meet you, Katie." I hugged Thaddeus as his arms suddenly became wrapped around me. He embraced me like he'd known me all his life. This was a little uncomfortable, but I went with it. I'm happy Eric is finally letting me into his world; I just wish I knew what took so long. I now have a new brother-in-law and a niece. Eric was right; she is adorable. Miranda tugged at my dress as her big doe eyes looked up at me. She obviously wanted a hug or something, but I wanted to warn her first: this is Gucci sweetie, so stop tugging on me with your dirty little hands. "It was really good to meet you both."

That was Thad as he shook mine and Epiphany's hand. He, Miranda, and Courtney were about to vanish as quickly as they came into view. Just as they were cued up, they seemed to be prompted out; and just like that, they all disappeared. "Katie, I'll be back shortly; I want to walk Courtney, Thad, and Miranda out. This isn't an appropriate setting for a seven-year-old." "Eric . . ." I wanted to stop him. Say something that would make him stay. I wanted him to sit down next to me and relax for once, but he was already gone. Soon after I took my next breath, my heart jumped and landed in my kneecaps. I suddenly felt sick on the stomach, like I ate some bad tuna the night before or something. My intuitions landed in my stomach, resting comfortably next to the ache that had me almost doubled over. Something wasn't right, and I knew it. I could feel it. I could just feel it . . . "Katie, what's wrong?!" Epiphany jumped out of her seat and darted over to me. Her face looked concerned because she knew something was wrong with me. I felt like I was going to pass out. My breathing became heavy. My hands were trembling. My mouth felt like someone had stuffed cotton in my jaws. "Katie, sit down." I didn't want to sit down. I had to find Eric. I wanted him to explain to me what just happened. He introduced me to his head hygienist, Courtney, his brother Thaddeus, and his niece, Miranda—what other explanations did I need? I was fully aware of what just occurred, but something isn't sitting right. My insides are telling me so. "Oh no, Katie! Kate, get up!" Epiphany screeched when I hit the floor. I lay there shaking uncontrollably. I couldn't stop. Sweat poured from my pores, and I'm almost sure foam just rolled down my cheek after it escaped my mouth. "Someone, please, help me! HELP!" Poor Epiphany, she was frantic. "Katie, help is coming, sweetie, okay. Just hold on!"

Chapter Twenty-Two

COURTNEY

"I've heard so much about you." That was Katie. She spoke as we shook hands after Erik introduced us. I hoped she wasn't waiting for a same here from me because I knew nothing about her. Erik never even mentioned her before the day he was shouting at her on his phone. "Courtney, Shaun, there is someone else I would like for you two to meet." Shaun had made his way upstairs with us. "Courtney, this is my brother Thaddeus; we all call him Thad for short." Erik's eyes shot downward. "And this is his daughter, my adorable niece, Miranda." She was the cutest little thing ever. Her dad wasn't too shabby, either. Before I could extend my hand to him, Thaddeus's arms were wrapped around me. And then there was his daughter, Miranda. She jerked at my pant leg, looking up at me. I instantly reached down and picked her up. "Well, hi there. How old are you, Miranda?" Before she could answer, Thad rushed her from my arms. "We really need to be going. It was nice meeting both of you."

Thaddeus, Miranda, and Erik all followed Katie's bulky body back down the staircase. She didn't look like a typical Fenmore's patron. She had an odd appearance, an odd walk, she wore odd clothes, and she even had an odd smell. Erik deemed her as his right hand earlier, but she didn't look much like a hygienist that would be running a swank dentist office for the Great Falls, Potomac elite. I don't discriminate, but no employee of mine would ever leave their homes looking how Katie showed up here this evening, regardless if they were on Fenmore's dime or not. "Erik, where are you going?" I tried to catch him before he walked off. When he turned to me, he said, "I'm just going to walk them to the door. Katie is not feeling well, and this is not exactly the atmosphere for a seven-year-old child." "Well, when you come back in, I'll be downstairs." "Okay . . . Give me just a few seconds." I nodded as Erik headed down the small staircase. "What?" Shaun had been staring at me since Erik left. "Why are you looking at me like that?" "Girl, what just happened?" I snapped, "What part did you miss?" "Who were those people?" I was quickly becoming annoyed. "Shaun, Erik introduced you to his assistant, his brother, and his brother's daughter at the same time he introduced me. What part did you miss?" "Obviously, you're the one that missed everything, including how bizarre Erik was acting. What was that all about?" When I didn't answer him, Shaun came back with, "Come on, Byrd; now I know you could tell something wasn't right with him. And you told me he didn't have a brother. Where did this Thaddeus person come from all of a sudden? He wasn't at the wedding, and neither was his daughter.

None of Erik's family or friends was at the wedding. Can you explain that?" My back teeth were grinding together so tight I'm sure Shaun could hear them. "Courtney, . . . Listen . . . You know I'm your friend, and I love you to death. I just want what's best for you. I've always told you that." His voice was calm and sweet; it's just too bad he was saying all the wrong things. "If constantly questioning Erik's motives and his actions are considered wanting what's best for me, then, girl, I'll pass." He looked offended. "Really, Courtney?" "Shaun, you were the one that was running around here just a few hours ago yapping about my husband being too secretive. 'Where is his family? 'Why haven't we met any extensions of him?' Now, after we meet not only an employee—a longtime employee might I add, his brother and his niece, you're still not satisfied." "Courtney, stop. Where the hell did he find those people? Don't you think his family and office assistant would have been at the man's wedding?" "Shaun, . . ." I wasn't shouting this time, but I'm sure my tone was heard in the near distance. "I know you love me. There is not a doubt in my mind about that. I know you care about what happens to me, but this . . . this problem you have with Erik has got to stop!" When I asked him, "Are you jealous of Erik and me?" his face lit up, and not in a good way. "Jealous? Courtney Byrd, chile, please! Erik is a very handsome man; anyone within twenty feet of him can see that. He dresses nice, he smells good, and from what you've led on, he's a stellar lover, but he's your man. Yours! You have a great life, Courtney. Some would even say you have a perfect life, but your life is perfect for you, not me. I have my own situations going on.

Furthermore, I've never been the jealous type. You know that." "He's my husband!" Now I was yelling. "What?" "You said Erik was 'My man.' He's not my man; he's my husband!" I was seconds away from calling Shaun the B-word. He hated being called a bitch almost as much as I hated being called girl. "Courtney, I don't give a damn about you getting mad. You snapped on me earlier about Erik, and now you're trying me again? I'm just looking out for you, but if you want to keep pretending something isn't off with your husband, honey be my guest. This damn man brings a pair of actors to your bar and introduces them to you as his family, and you stand here coming for me when I question why? Girl, stop! You can keep acting like something isn't off with Eric, but don't get mad when I call bullshit when I see bullshit." Now my blood was boiling! "Did you just say, actors? What the fuck! Shaun, I think something is wrong with you, not Erik!" "Courtney, Erik doesn't even favor that man or his little girl. And why did he wait until now to introduce you, if that's what you want to call it? They all ran out two minutes after they got up here." That's it! I had to get away from Shaun before my fist landed between his shiny lips. Actors? Was he serious? "Courtney, wait!" he grabbed my arm. I snatched away from him. "I'm done with this conversation, Shaun!" I looked around to make sure no one was watching as I hushed my tone. "I don't know where all this sudden animosity for Erik is coming from, but I'm not doing this with you tonight." I couldn't stand to look at Shaun for another second. He was way out of line this time, and there was no coming back. "Courtney, I know what I saw, because you saw it too. I'm not about to stand here and let him make a fool out of you, Court—" Shaun was cut off by the shouting female voice coming from behind us. It was one of my hostesses that finally decided to show up. "Courtney . . ." She was panting for air. "What is it, Angela?" "On the other side . . . The other side of . . . where we are now, second-second level, a woman just fainted!" "Fainted?" That was Shaun. "Fainted?" That was me. "Yes, she fainted. I'm not sure what happened, but she looks pretty bad . . . the ambulance is already here."

Chapter Twenty-Three

KATIE

When my eyes awoke, I felt peaceful. My heart seemed to be beating at a normal pace again. My body wasn't tight and tensed like it was when I got here, and I'm sure the foaming stopped. I was still half-asleep but fully aware of everything that had happened last night, where I was now, and why. "Hey Katie, you're awake . . ." It was Epiphany. I knew she would be here, but Kyle? Why was she here? I didn't want that bitch to see me like this. On second thought, I don't care what she thinks. I don't care what Epiphany thinks. I don't care what anyone thinks anymore. After what happened at Fenmore's last night, I'm finally ready to admit I have a problem. Or shall I say my husband has a problem? There is definitely something wrong. I can feel it in my heart, and so can my sisters. That's why they're both looking at me like my body is about to shatter right in front of them. "I'm okay." I rolled over, so my back was to them. I didn't want to look at them. I didn't want to answer the questions written on their faces. I just wanted to be left alone. I wanted to fall back asleep, and when I awakened this time, last night would be part of a dream that I'd never have to relive again. "Do you want some water?" "Epiphany, I said I'm fine." "Katie, will you look at me and tell me what happened last night." I sat up in the small, hard hospital bed. With my sisters here—and the morning sun shining through the drape-less windows—it was clear I wasn't going to get any more rest. "The doctor hasn't been in yet this morning. They ran tests when she first got here." "It was just a panic attack!" Just because I'm in a hospital bed doesn't mean I was helpless. I could speak for myself. I didn't need Epiphany explaining anything to Kyle. Besides, it was nothing but a panic attack, gosh. Kyle asked, "Where is Eric now?" "I'm right here." My husband was standing in the doorway of my room. He didn't make his presence known to Kyle or Epiphany because we all jumped at the same instance from the sound of his voice. "Kyle, . . . Epiphany, I want to speak with Eric alone, please." I could tell from the look on their faces, especially Kyle's, they didn't want to leave me. They were so protective of me as if I needed protection. Well, I didn't. What I need is to speak with my husband in private. Kyle looked at Eric, then back down to me. I didn't realize it, but she'd been holding my hand since I woke up. "We'll be right outside that door." I nodded for them to leave. And they did without connecting eyes with Eric. He came closer to me as I sat there with my arms folded across my chest. I didn't speak even though I wanted to. I had queries that only he could answer like why was he here now? Today is Thursday. He always leaves me on Wednesdays. Then there was the incident at Fenmore's last night. I want to know who were those people he introduced me to? His brother, niece, and hygienist came out of thin air. I knew Eric one year before we married, yet I never even heard him mention a brother or niece. His story was always the same: Mother and Father were killed when he was ten; he was sent to a home for boys, left that home when he turned eighteen and got a scholarship into The University of Maryland School of Medicine. I took his story to be true; now, I don't know what to believe. He asked, "What are you doing?" as I pressed the little red button on the cord lying next to me as hard as I could. I needed my sisters more than I ever imagined I would. I needed Kyle and Epiphany to save me from this man staring down at me. Rescue me from any more of his shenanigans. Just get me out of this bed, away from this hospital, and far away from him! "Yes, Mrs. Reynolds?" I wanted to cry as I spoke into the intercom, but I held back the tears. "Nurse, can you send my sisters back in here, please?" I knew they were right outside my door, but I didn't want to alarm them by yelling out into the hallway. "Yes, Mrs. Reynolds, I'll send them right in." "Why are you calling for your sisters?" "Eric, I think you should leave." "Leave? What-what did I do?" I didn't answer him. "Katie?" Now I wouldn't look at him. "Would you please talk to me?" Nope. "Katie . . . look at me." I wouldn't. "Katie, please." Come on Kyle and Epiphany, hurry . . . "Katie, why are you—" "Katie, is everything okay?" Epiphany came into the room first. "Katie, what is it?" Kyle came charging in after her. They were both heading right for me, which meant my husband would soon be heading out. "Why are you doing this to me?" I could hear the desperation in Eric's voice as he spoke. "Katie, what did I do?" "Eric, I think you should leave." My little sister was always there when I needed her to be. She was saying the words to my husband I was afraid to say. Her body language was sharp and bitter just as mine would be if I had more strength. She was strong for me. She was angry for me. She did exactly what I needed her to do without any verbal orders from me. "Katie, what is this about? I don't understand why you're doing this!" "This is about Katie not wanting to talk to you right now, Eric! She wants you to leave." It was Kyle's turn to stand up to Eric man-to-man. I love my sisters. "Would someone please tell me what the hell is going on? I'm not going anyplace until I get some answers." "Eric," back to Epiphany, "lower your voice. This is a hospital." My husband looked back down at me. "Do you want me to leave, Katie?" When my answer stalled, he said, "I asked you a question. Do you want me to leave?" I didn't know what to say. My sisters were on my right, glaring over at my husband with him on my left glaring down at me. "Katie?" "Yes, Eric, I think you should go." "Why are you doing this? Just tell me what I've done?" "Katie, I'm calling security. Dr. Reynolds needs to go now!" Kyle's sarcasm flew across the room. "Kyle, this is between Katie and me!" "Yeah, and she asked you to leave!

"Everyone stop! Please, just stop fighting." I took a deep breath. "Kyle, Epiphany, give me five more minutes alone with Eric; I shouldn't have called you guys back in here so soon." "Katie, you don't want him here, that's why you called us back in here so soon." "Epiphany, five minutes." I could tell she didn't want to leave. Neither did Kyle, but I had to speak with my husband alone once more. "We'll be right down the hall when you're ready." I waited for Kyle and Epiphany to leave the room to say what I had to say to Eric. "Katie . . . I don't get this. Why are you and your sisters treating me this way? What have I done?" "Something doesn't feel right, Eric. Something is just not sitting well with me." I asked, "Why did you take me to that place last night?" "I told you, my receptionist—" "I know what you told me, but . . . Eric, who is Courtney?" "Courtney is the head hygienist at my practice. I already told you that too." "Who is Thaddeus?" He breathed heavily before he said, "Thaddeus is my older brother. We're four years apart." "Who is Miranda? And don't say your niece, because I'm not buying it. Just like I'm not buying this, Thad person is your older brother. Just tell me the truth, Eric. For once, don't lie to me. Stop trying to control every single piece of content in our marriage, and just talk to me. Be honest with me." My words were coming out beyond my control. "I sit there in that house all the time waiting for you, wondering what you're doing. Who you're with? What you're eating? What kind of cologne you're wearing? I sit and wonder because I don't know. You're always away, and that's so unfair to me, Eric. I am your wife! I need you more than just a few days a week, can't you see that?" All the muscles in my face collapsed as I started breaking down. "You have me on this schedule that I just can't take anymore." He stood there quiet. "And would you say something! I'm about to lose my mind, and all you can do is stand there blank? Say something!" I sniffled before I reached for a tissue. "Katie . . . Katie, how could you say those things?" His voice was low and raspy. "Because, Eric, it's all true, and-and it's killing me." "You had a panic attack last night, Katie. A panic-attack. I had nothing to do with that." "You don't think so?" "No, I don't. And for you to lie there and make accusations about my family, and colleague is outrageous!" "You want to talk outrageous? If I wasn't in this hospital bed right now, where would you be? Huh? Let's hear it, Eric. Where-would-you-be!" When he didn't answer, I screamed, "Exactly! You wouldn't be with me. You wouldn't be at our home. You wouldn't even be a phone call away. You never are unless it's our designated time to be together. That's what's outrageous!" More tears streamed out of my eyes as my bottled-up feelings poured from my lips. "I can't do this anymore, Eric. I can't be your wife Sunday through Wednesday, or whenever you decide to come back home. I just can't . . . I won't." "Katie, I'm a doctor!" "That's funny—that's not what the private investigator said." Oh God, I didn't mean to say that! Shit! Shit! Shit! I wasn't going to bring the PI up to him, at least not this way. I went too far . . . I could tell Eric was fuming before any of his angered words left his mouth. "Wait-a-fucking-minute! You hired a private investigator?"

"No, I didn't." "So, who did? Your nosey, miserable sisters? Your parents, who you see maybe once a year? Who the hell did this, Katie?!" "Eric, this isn't about anybody but you. You and those people from last night." "I told you who those people were, and you're still sitting there accusing me of lying about my family?! You dirty bitch, how dare you?" When my eyes bugged out of my head, Eric came back with, "Yeah, I said it...You are a dirty, wicked, coldhearted, lowdown bitch for that. It's your family that should be questioned and scrutinized, not mine, Katie! And you wonder why it's taken me so long to bring them around." Eric's eyes were starting to scare me. He didn't look like the same man I fell in love with. He didn't even look like the same man that walked into this room a few minutes ago. Even the tone of his voice had changed. The look in his face was now wild and vicious. His fists were balled up. His teeth gritted in his jaws. His mouth had formed a complete circle from anger. "You listen to me, Katie Morgan, and you listen good because I will not say this more than once. You pull whatever private investigator off me before I make you, your fat-ass sisters, and your distant parents all disappear. You don't wanna fuck with me, bitch." I didn't know what to say or how to react. Eric has never spoken to me this way before. "Eric, how dare you call me those names! You don't speak to me that way; I don't care how mad you are!" "Oh, you better care how mad I am . . . your fucking life depends on it." "That's it! I'm calling security!" Before I could reach for the red button on top of the long tan chord, Eric threatened, "If you call security in here, I will bury you alive under our house." He reached down and fisted my hospital gown. "Look at my face." He stared into my eyes. "I hope you can tell that I'm serious." Eric yanked me back before he turned and headed for the door. I sat there, trembling until he was gone. I was so scared I didn't move. I didn't blink. I just sat there, shaking. I didn't know that man that just left . . . I didn't recognize him or his threats. Eric would never talk to me that way. He wouldn't call me a bitch and threaten to bury me alive. Whoever that man was, I'm glad he's gone. When Kyle and Epiphany came through the door, I quickly warned, "If you haven't pulled that PI off Eric, please do so right now. Please!" I thought my life, and theirs depends on it . . .

Chapter Twenty-Four

COURTNEY

"Erik, you startled me." I was standing in front of my husband butt naked, running a fluffy white bath towel over my wet body. I wasn't expecting him to be home still. Usually, he takes off like a thief in the night early every Sunday morning, so I was really shocked to see him still in bed after I showered. "Courtney, if I was leaving, you don't think I would go without saying goodbye, do you?" I said, "I would hope not," even though I was thinking, it's not like you haven't done it before. Erik was lying in our bed shirtless with the comforter pulled up to his waist. I wonder if he's still naked? "So, what's on your agenda for the rest of the day, Court?" I wrapped the towel around my waist as I headed for the bed. I sat down, kissed Erik's succulent, juicy, moist lips before I answered, "Shopping. Shaun and I need to pick up a few things for Fenmore's before tomorrow night." "So, you and Shaun are speaking again? You know babe, you've said some pretty nasty things about him these last few weeks." I rolled my eyes. "I know, and he deserved every bit of it, but we're okay for now. As long as he tries his best to stay out of my business, I will try my best not to fire him." "What were you two fighting about anyway?" I paused for a second. "It doesn't matter . . . much about nothing." I got up and headed to my side of the closet to get dressed. When Erik came up behind me, his hands landed on my bare shoulders. "Courtney, . . . I'm ready." I turned around to him. "You're ready for what?" He turned and walked toward the window. "I want a family of my own, baby. I want to be a dad." He turned back around to me. "I love our life, Court, but-well, sometimes I feel like something is missing." He rushed over to me. "You fulfill me in ways I never even imagined possible, but . . . babe, there is still an empty hole inside of me. I-I have everything I've ever wanted in life except a baby." I didn't know what to say. I was completely taken aback. And where is all this coming from? Why now? I'm not ready for this . . . We are defiantly not ready for this. "Tell me what's on your mind, Courtney. I can see the uneasiness in your face. Talk to me, tell me how you feel." "I don't know how I feel. I-I wasn't expecting this. A baby? Erik, come on. I just opened my business; you know that. Since Fenmore's, I'm never home . . . and neither are you." "Court, you know I'm working." "You're always working, Erik. And so am I, so when are we going to have time to raise a new baby?" "Babe, career parents make it work every day." I went back to the closet. "Erik, can we talk about this later?" I started pulling clothes off hangers. "This is a big step, and I can't stand here and give you the answers you're waiting to hear." I looked at him as I put my jeans on. "I love you, and I want to have kids with you someday, but not like this." His eyebrows furred when he asked, "Not like what?" "Erik, don't go there. I may be able to wait for days without even hearing from you, but a baby cannot." "Courtney, I'll . . . I'll work on my schedule. I'll change hours . . . I'll-I'll change days around so I'm here more. Just like now . . . I'm here. You thought I was gone earlier, but I'm right here." "Well, what happens tomorrow when you're not? What happens when I try to reach you and can't? A baby can't have half a dad, Erik." My emotions started running high. "I want to spend the rest of my life with you. I want to continue to make you happy. I want to fulfill your every desire, but I need more from you." "And I'm prepared to give you more, babe. I promise. I'll be a better husband . . . Court, I'll be a better man." When he handed me a pamphlet, I asked, "What's this?" "It's for Children's Choice; I went there last week and spoke with an advisor. I got some information along with that pamphlet." "Adoption? Erik, I don't know what to say." "Courtney, there is no one else in this world for me. You know that. I want to spend my life with you." He took the pamphlet from me. "Say you'll take this step with me. Say you'll raise a child with me." "We can work on . . . adopting. But, Erik, I can't do this alone. I can't even do this with you here half the time. I want a family with you, Erik . . . but only with all of you." "Yes, Courtney . . . You have my word; I'll do better." Our bodies crashed together. "Thank you, Courtney. Thank you so much. Thank you . . . God, I thank you . . ." If we had an audience, I'm sure there wouldn't be a single dry eye in the place after watching us. When Erik reached down and kissed my lips, it was as if he'd lit a torch inside of me. I was on fire for my husband with our happiness turning into heightened ecstasy. My breath became lost with his. We become one as our passion ignited to a level neither one of us could control. When we made it to the bed, my legs rested on his shoulders as his manhood found the entrance to my world. I moaned as all of Erik's inches pressed inside of me. I reached around to grab for his plump ass that waded in the warm air as he made love to me. I threw my head back as his tongue feathered around my neck. "Erik! Oh, yes . . . Right there . . ." He was driving me crazy. Erik pounded me in every position he flipped me into. He was so dominant and strong, commanding every part of my body all with the strength of his manhood. Once we finished, I cuddled up on his smooth, buffed chest. "I love you, Erik." "I love you too, Court. I love you more than anything in this world." "I believe that because I feel the same way about you." After we kissed, I laid my head back down to Erik's chest waiting and welcoming the next chapter in our marriage: a new baby . . .

Chapter Twenty-Five

KATIE

He didn't come home early Sunday morning, as he usually does. He didn't come back last night, and he's not here now. I haven't heard from Eric since he threatened me and stormed out of my hospital room over a week ago. He hasn't tried to reach out to me since that day, and I damn sure wasn't reaching out to him. I didn't know where he was, and I didn't care. He had no right to threaten violence on my family or me. I never thought he was that kind of man; I always thought he was perfect. Not a monster that would say the things he said to me that day. When I got to the kitchen, I picked up the Vicodin tablet sitting next to my glass. I popped it in my mouth and splashed red wine to the back of the dry throat to wash it down. Booze and pills were the only things that seemed to be keeping me sane. On my trip out to the pool, I caught a glimpse of myself in the hallway mirror as I passed by. I stopped and did a triple take just to make sure the image floating by was me. I no longer recognized myself.

I had no idea who the pale face staring back at me belong to. She had dark circles under her eyes. Worry in her face—loneliness in her spirit. I asked, "What is wrong with me?" as my wine glass went crashing onto the walnut parquet floor. I wanted to spit as my eyes revealed my image in the mirror. I would rather go blind than to look at myself for another second. I went into the half bath and grabbed my wooden handle hairbrush from the sink. I ran back out to the hallway to see if my reflection had changed. I went to the mirror, praying fear wasn't still etched all over my vacant face, but it was still there. Worse than before. I couldn't stand to look into my eyes for another minute, so I slammed the handle of the hairbrush into the mirror. I kept hitting the mirror until the last piece of glass made it to the floor. I cried as I stared around my immaculate home. Everything was perfectly in order, not broken and dark like me. As I stood in the lavished living area, I thought about running a broken piece of glass over my wrist and end it all. I might as well because I have no life without Eric. I can't start over; I'm not capable of living a healthy, happy life without him. It would be too painful, and I wasn't accustomed to pain. The easy route would be to kill myself; I just want to close my eyes and never wake up. Now I was crying hysterically. I couldn't control myself. I was in such agony, and I just wanted it to end. I wanted it all to stop. I wanted this hurt to go away so I could rest. When I picked up one of the broken pieces of glass down by my feet, my hand started to rain blood after I carved open a big chunk of flesh. I screamed and bolted through the house from pain. Once I made it to the kitchen, I plopped down in the middle of the floor, holding my bloody arm. In-between the excruciating pain in my hand, all I could do was ponder my life and what a mess it was: No degree. No career. No children. And now, no Eric. What a joke! I couldn't do anything right. "Katie, my God, KATIE! What happened to you?" Eric charged toward me when he came into the kitchen from the garage. He was more alarmed than I was with the souls of his shoes slipping around in my blood as he tried to get to me. "Katie, I'm calling an ambulance!" When he went for his phone, I stopped him. "Don't please . . . I don't want our street crawling with fire trucks and rescue squads. I don't want anyone to think something is wrong in here." I was in so much pain I felt as if I would blackout at any moment. "Katie, there is something wrong, look at you." He looked down at all the glass. "What happened?" He asked, "What did you do?" now looking right at me. "Eric, . . . I don't know . . . I don't remember." I was so woozy I could barely speak. Eric got up to grab a few towels and to call nine-one-one after I begged him not to. My voice was only one octave above a whisper when I said, "Eric, I love you." "Here, put this around your arm." He held my arm up as the dispatcher told him to do. "You don't love me anymore. I can see it in your face. You don't . . .Oh, Eric." "Is that what this is about? You hurt yourself because you think I don't love you anymore? Katie, I am a busy doctor. You knew that when I married you. I love you with all my heart and soul, but you and your sisters cannot bring a PI into our marriage. That's not how this works. Not with me." I could hear the sirens from the ambulance in the short distance. "Eric, I didn't know what to do, where to turn. You leave me here with access to any and everything I want except-you. Why . . . why can't I have you, Eric? I need you . . . the man I married. Not . . . not a man that is constantly abandoning me. And surely not a man that would call me a wicked bitch." Eric looked away from me when I spit his words back out to him. "I'm not a wicked bitch; I'm just a woman desperate for her marriage to work." "Katie, this is not the time. You're hurt, and you need to get to a hospital." I begged, "Eric, please just tell me . . . What is out there that keeps you away from me? I know it's not just your practice . . . it's not your patients . . . what is it? Who is it? Who is out there, Eric? It's something or somebody that takes you away from me." When the doorbell chimed, Eric went to get up from the floor, but I grabbed his shirt. "Just tell me, Eric. Tell me . . . who's out there? Who is it? . . ."

Chapter Twenty-Six

COURTNEY

Two Months Later . . . "Courtney, are you nervous?" "I am, but I'll be okay." Erik and I were sitting in the adoption agency's waiting room. Today was our first meeting to get the process started to adopt our child. In a few short weeks, we'll have our new baby girl. I had my heart set on a little boy, but Erik did everything except insist we got a girl. Once we have her, I thought we would name her Anna after my mom, or Lucy after my grandmother. As long as the name we choose doesn't affect her getting a good job, or into a good school, I'm okay with it. I looked over at Erik. "How are you feeling over there?" "Courtney, do you know how long I've wanted a baby? I'm over the moon right now." I'm glad he was so happy because I'm a nervous wreck! I don't know the first thing about being a parent, and neither does Erik. What I do know is we have a lot of love to give, and hopefully that will be enough. I've been practicing that line all morning. "Give me your hand." I reached my sweaty hand toward Erik's awaiting palm. "Courtney, your hand is ice-cold." "I know, but I'm okay." I tried to play it off, but no, I'm not okay. "No, you're not. You're shaking." I finally confessed, "Erik, I'm terrified." "Don't be, babe. I'm right here with you. We're going to do this together." "But what if . . . What if I'm not a good dad? What if I skip a doctor's appointment? Or forget the baby's feeding times? What if I forget to change her, or I don't get all the air out of her tummy when I burp her?" Erik chuckled under his breath. "Most babies don't let you forget things like that." "Erik, I'm serious." "Court, listen, we're going to make great parents, okay. What doesn't come to us naturally, we'll learn. A baby is a huge step, but we'll have all we need within each other." "I hope you're right." I'm still petrified at just the thought of what we were about to do. I just want to do a good job. Show Erik, Shaun, Mama, and myself that I can do this. I've always been successful at pretty much everything I've set my mind to, so hopefully, raising a child won't be any different. "You know Court when I was a little boy, I always dreamt of being two things when I grew up." "Really?" I asked, "What?" "I've always wanted to be a doctor and a dad. I would imagine myself leaving home wearing my long white coat ready to start my day. But first, I would kiss my beautiful wife, then play with my little girl for a few minutes right before heading off into the world. That's been my dream for so long, and now it's about to come true." He squeezed my hand. "And Courtney don't worry; I'm going to do whatever it takes to make it work. I want to be a dad, and I only want this with you. I need you, Courtney. I can't do this without you." "And you won't have to because I'm right here." I took a deep breath. "We'll get through this . . . together." "We have a few forms for you guys to fill out to get the ball rolling." The small stature female coming toward us with a clipboard interrupted our moment. "Once you two fill these forms out, you can go back and meet Mrs. Moss, familiarize yourself with the adoption process, and move on to the next phase." I wanted to ask her what the next phase was, but I kept quiet, smiled, and nodded. "Here you are." She handed the clipboard to Erik. "Take your time, relax, and let me know when you two are ready." "Yes, ma'am, thank you." Erik was so polite. "Well, this is it." I smiled and shook my head for him to start the forms. He smiled back at me before focusing his attention on the papers in his lap. For some reason, he hesitated before answering the first question, which was Name. "Erik, what is it?" I was confused. "Huh? . . . Oh, nothing. Just a few butterflies, that's all. I'm cool." He looked back down at the forms and proceeded to answer question one. Next to Name, he prints his first name ever so gently E-R-I-K. Then he writes my name next to his. I watched his every move as if it would be his last, cosigning to make sure everything was accurate. Once again, he pauses when it's time to write the baby's expected name in the appropriate field. The form called for three choices, but Erik only wrote one name: K-A-T-I-E. I stopped him. "What the hell do you think you're doing? You cannot be serious. We are not naming our daughter Katie!" "Courtney, why are you acting this way? Katie was my grandmother's name." I had my mouth opened, but no more words followed. I thought his grandmother's name was

Katie? I've never heard him mention a grandmother before. I would have remembered that. I wanted to ask more questions, but my nerves—and all the caseworkers buzzing around—kept my mouth closed. When Erik handed me the form to sign, I signed my name and handed the clipboard back to him. The adoption process was underway. Soon Erik and I will be parents, but I still want to know why does he want to name our new daughter Katie? . . .

Chapter Twenty-Seven

KATIE

I panted as I sprinted into the sunroom with a Demi Lovato track blaring through my earbuds. I went out for a lovely morning jog on the trail near our home before the sun came up. I took off my Nike sportswear jacket and laid it on the chair in the kitchen. It's nearly seventy degrees out already, but I wore it to make sure my bandaged arm stayed covered. As I ran the trail, I didn't want any of my snobby neighbors to think my husband beats me, nor did I want them to think I sliced my arm up because he wouldn't come home. My appearance must, at all times, appear perfect no matter how messed up I really am on the inside. All ninety-three stitches dissolved, but my cuts were still healing under my carefully wrapped, hidden bandages. Just as I was toweling off my petite frame, I heard the front door open. "Hey, Katie." It was Eric. When he laid his briefcase down, he came over and hugged me. Once I gave him a weak, one arm hug, I went over to the refrigerator. He said, "No, I'm okay" when I asked if he wanted something to drink. Since the day I cut myself up, Eric has been home a lot more. Lately, he's been attentive to me and every one of my needs. He's completely reverted to the man I fell in love with, but I'm not letting my guards down. Uh-huh, not this time. That day when we were on the floor surrounded by the blood that was pouring from my arm, I begged him to tell me what goes on in his life when he leaves me; where does he go, what does he do? I asked him who else was out there waiting for him, but all I got was work. "Katie, there is something I want to talk to you about." I took a seat at the island. "Okay . . . what is it, Eric?" He took a few deep breaths. "Katie . . . Katie, I've been thinking about this for some time now. I want a baby. I think we're ready." I instantly leaped up and wrapped my arms around him tight. I can't remember the last time I held my husband this close. I was so excited as I bounced up and down in his arms. "A baby, Eric? I didn't think you were ready." I sure am. "This is such a big step for us." Being pregnant wouldn't be horrible, right? There is the morning sickness, the swelling, the dark spots, and the weight gain. I'm willing to temporarily lose my tiny waist to carry my husband's child. I'll just make Epiphany rub me down three times a week with a few gallons of cocoa butter to control the stretch marks as I'm sure she does for her own flabby body every other day. "This is a big step, baby, but I feel it's one we're ready for. I want a family of my own, Katie. I want to be a dad." He took my hands into his. "I love our life, babe, but-well, sometimes I feel like something is missing. You fulfill me in ways I never even imagined possible, but . . . Katie, there is still an empty hole inside of me. I-I have everything I've ever wanted except a baby." I didn't hesitate when I told him how ready I am. I've wanted to carry Eric's baby—remember, more than ten if he wanted me to—since the day we met. This will be a good thing; hopefully, solve most of our problems. A baby will reconnect what I thought was gone between us, which is exactly what we need. Eric is already making changes in his schedule to spend more time at home, so this is perfect timing. "So, you're ready for this? . . . are we having a baby?" His face lit up like a child on Christmas Eve. "Yes, Eric." I was crying like I did the night he proposed. "Yes, I want to have a baby. This is the right time." "It is . . . It's our time. With this Katie, you have made me the happiest man on the planet." Now he was crying, too. "Thank you. Thank you so much for agreeing to this, Katie. Thank you . . . God, I thank you!" Eric was wrapped in my arms as if I had just given him the world. Maybe I had. I could tell he wanted this, and I was prepared to give him a baby. He finally rose out of my cuddle and looked into my eyes. "Katie, do you love me?" "Of course, I do." "Do you trust me?" I looked away from him. "Eric . . ." "Katie, do you trust me? I mean, do you trust me to be a good dad?" I looked back into his eyes. "I know you will be an excellent father. You are a great husband and a good man. If our child turns out to be half the person you are, he or she will be fortunate." "Do you mean that?" There go those child's eyes again. "Yes, I mean it. You have all the qualities I want in the father of my child." "I'm going to do a good job, Katie. You'll see. I'm going to be a good dad to our son. I won't let you down. I promise." "I know, you won't let me down, Eric." I hugged him. "I can't wait until our son or daughter gets here." "No, Katie, you mean our son. We're going to have a boy." "Well, Eric . . ." I laughed. "I don't think we're the ones who decide that, hon." "We will have a son, Katie. Just watch." He lay his head back down on my breast. "We're going to have a strong, handsome, precious little boy. And you know what we're going to name him?" I kissed his forehead right before I asked, "What are we going to name our son, Poppa?" My heart dived into a place deep inside of me; so deep, I couldn't catch it or my breath. When my husband's mouth formed the name, "Courtney," I didn't know how to respond. All I could do was stand there frozen, locked inside of my own skin. Right then, it seemed all the twisted, confused, muddled emotions I felt that night at Fenmore's were back. I feel like I'm going to pass out right here, just like I did that night. The tension in my chest is back. The palpitations are too. And the questions for my husband were surely back starting with his fascination with Courtney!

Chapter Twenty-Eight

COURTNEY

"Thanks again for coming out with me today, Shaun. I didn't want to shop by myself." Shaun and I were driving down Thirty-Second Street coming back from a baby boutique downtown. I was kind of surprised when Shaun agreed to come baby shopping with me. Since I told him Erik and I are about to adopt a child, he's been very quiet and distant. If it wasn't about the bar, he and I didn't really have much to say to each other. I can tell he forces himself to seem happy for Erik and me, but his face tells how he truly feels every time he tries to fake it with me. Honestly, I can care less about how he feels. I love my husband. I trust him. We're having a new baby, and that will be that. On second thought . . . "Shaun, you're my best friend." My head bobbed between him and the road. "Talk to me . . . I may not want to hear what you have to say, but just say it already. You've been so fake lately, and I can't take it anymore."

"Courtney, look, honey, if you're happy, then I'm happy for you. And you're right; you are my best friend, and all I want is the best for you." "Erik makes me happy, Shaun; you know that better than anyone." "Oh okay, cool . . . so does that mean he's coming home more?" Here we go. Mm-hmm, that's what I was waiting for. Bring it on, bitch! "Have you heard anything else about his hygienist, brother or niece? Of course, you haven't, and I know that bothers you, Byrd." I shook my head the whole time Shaun was talking. "Erik hasn't changed, and a baby isn't going to change him. I've been holding it all in, so you don't get mad at me, but I just hate what he's putting you through." I spat, "And what the fuck is he putting me through, Shaun?!" "Well, shit, you tell me! How many nights a week does he come home? Or is it easier for you to count the nights that he doesn't? Girl, I know he's a doctor, but damn. His patients only need him on certain days and nights of the week?" I wanted to slam on the breaks in hopes Shaun would go flying through the windshield, but no such luck; he's wearing his seatbelt. Damnit! I should have never asked for his opinion. Why didn't I just let him keep his mouth closed, because now he won't shut up. "Shaun, I'm not going there with you. I don't have to discuss my husband's schedule with you or anyone else who doesn't pay the bills in my home. God, why can't you just be happy for me? If I'm not questioning Erik, neither should you. Just let me handle it, Shaun. Look . . . I need you right now probably more than ever because I'm so scared. You know we're about to have a new baby; can you please just be there for me?" He sighed when he crossed his arms. "I'm here, Courtney. I may have some reservations about Erik, but I'm going to be here for you regardless." Good, because I didn't need this from him right now. In a few hours, Erik and I are going to meet our baby for the first time, so I need his support, not his opinions. Not today. Not when my hands are starting to tremble so badly, I can hardly grip the wheel. "Byrd, I love you, and I will always be here for you; you know that." "I know. And I love you too, but trust me; trust us, everything is fine . . ." Two Hours Later . . . Once I dropped Shaun off, I headed home, so Erik and I could ride to the adoption agency together. Today is the day we pick out our brand-new baby girl. We can't bring her home for another couple of weeks, but today we get to meet the baby we plan to make our own. I can't wait to see her little eyes looking up at me, or feel her soft skin resting against mine. I just want to hold her in my arms and tell her how much I already love her. As I walk into the house, I wonder if I'll make a good father. Will I be a positive role model? Will I be able to teach our daughter right from wrong without going for a wire hanger the way Faye Dunaway did in Mommie Dearest? I've done tons of research, read dozens of parenting guides and books, and I think I've signed up for at least two hundred parent support groups to help me along the way. Other than that, I guess I'll have to rely on my instincts: instincts and a couple of hundred phone calls to Mama, that is. "Hey, baby." Erik looked up at me when I walked into our bedroom. "Hey." I bent down and kissed him, sitting on the bed. He asked, "How are you feeling?" "I'm fine, just a little nervous . . ." I gave him the screwface when I asked, "Erik, why aren't you dressed?" He was sitting there wearing boxers and a tank with his suit hanging on the outside of our closet door. "I'm not going." "What do you mean you're not going? Today is the day we meet our daughter." When he didn't respond, I asked, "Erik, did you forget?" I went and grabbed his suit. "You need to get dressed; the counselor already made it clear that we shouldn't miss, or be late, for any of our intake appointments." I held his suit out to him. "Here, put this on so we can go. We have to be there in less than an hour." "Court, . . . I said, I'm not going." I threw his suit down on the bed, still on the hanger. "Did you reschedule our appointment?" I started rolling my neck with attitude. "Erik, why didn't you tell me you rescheduled? I had two vendor meetings, and a bar staff interview that I moved around for our appointment today." "Courtney, I didn't reschedule." His eyes looked up to me when he said, "I'm just not going . . . And neither are you." "Wait-what? Why not? What are you talking about?" I got nothing from him. "Erik?!" "Courtney, we're not going because I've already met our daughter. I went last week and spoke with Mrs. Moss." "Erik, wait . . ." I tried to catch my tone. "You spoke with Mrs. Moss about what?" "I asked her if it would be okay if we moved the process up a week." "We? You did that without talking to me first?" "Courtney, I just wanted to hold our little girl. I just had to meet her. I had to hold her in my arms. Look into her precious little eyes. I couldn't wait any longer, so I just did it." "You're kidding, right? You have got to be fucking kidding me! Erik, how could you do this without me? Why didn't you just . . . why didn't you just tell me so that I could've gone with you? This makes me think you're hiding something from me!" I was furious. "Courtney, calm down. What would I be hiding from you?" "You tell me!" When Erik went to touch me, I slapped his hand away. "Having a child was our decision, Erik. Ours! This is going to be our child coming into our lives, living in our home! How could you make a decision that wasn't yours to make?" "Courtney, listen." He reached out for me again. "Don't you touch me! Don't you dare touch me! How could you do this, Erik?" I was screaming, "How could you do this?" when the question I should've been shouting at my husband was, Why did you do this? because I didn't understand. "Erik, why did you go down to that agency a week ahead of time without me?!" I saw red. "I WANT TO KNOW WHY!" "I-I don't know, Court . . . I guess I just-I couldn't control myself." When I shrieked, "You couldn't control yourself!" he just sat there looking as if he was searching for an explanation that wouldn't come to him. "What was the purpose, Erik? What was the reason?" He still didn't answer me. "You can't answer that because there wasn't a reason for you to go there without me. This was just another way for you to control me, this situation, and our marriage just like you try to control everything else." All he could say was, "Courtney, you're wrong," but I wasn't wrong. "I am so tired of you, Erik! I'm tired of this controlled, premeditated bullshit that you're always, always, ALWAYS putting me through! I'm tired, and I'm so done." I shot over to our closet and flung open the double wooden doors. I headed to the backdrop in search of my Gucci duffle. I'm getting out of here, and I'm leaving in style, honey. "Courtney, what are you doing?" He had some nerve to be calm. "Erik, what does it look like I'm doing? I can't take you anymore." I started flinging all my trousers off hangers. Then I went for my color-coordinated nits, then my suits, now my shoes. I grabbed as many shoes as I could fit in my bag. "I'm done, Erik. I put up with everything you dish out, and most time, I don't even complain. I just roll with it, but not anymore. This is my breaking point." He tried to stop me on my fourth trip from the closet. "Erik-move!" My back teeth were gritting together. "Courtney, you have to listen to me." "I said move, goddamn it!" I've never sworn so much in my life, at least not in one sitting. "Courtney, you can't leave me!" Oh, now he wants to show some emotion? "And why can't I? You don't need me. You do everything just fine on your own." "What is that supposed to mean? What are you talking about?" I threw down the bottle of Jean Paul Gaultier I just snatched from my vanity as I squared up with Erik. "I'm talking about how you picked out this house without me. How you went and purchased my Range Rover without me, assuming I'd love it just because it's big and expensive. And let's not forget the child that's all set to come into this house that I have yet to lay eyes on per your request." Erik slopped down on the bed in front of me. "This time-schedule that you have our lives on, all of the secrets . . . Erik, I just . . . I can't do this anymore. You know I love you, but this . . . this life is not for me. I didn't sign up for this. I want to spend the rest of my days with you, but sometimes I don't even know who you are. And quite frankly, I'm tired of trying to figure it out." He jumped up. "Courtney, please don't do this! Don't leave! I'm sorry, okay, baby. Please, I'm sorry." I picked up my shaken bottle of cologne and headed for my stuffed duffle bag. He could save all the apologizes because I'm over it. Now I was the calm one, while Erik was going ballistic. "Courtney, what about our marriage? What about our vows? Huh . . . What about the promise you made to me, Courtney? You promised me you would never leave me." I stopped in my tracks and peered back at Erik. "I was waiting for that . . . I was waiting for you to drag that promise up when it seemed convenient. I made a promise never to leave you, Erik, but what about the promises you made me? To honor me. To cherish me. To love me! Hell, to come home!" "You don't think I love you?" "I don't know what to think anymore." When Erik crashed back down to the bed, that was it, and just like that, I restarted packing to leave. I love him, but I cannot live like this. I can't, and I won't, and there was nothing he could do to change my mind. I think I made that clear. Erik let me leave our bedroom in peace. He sat there without any more objections as I zoomed around the room, rushing whatever I could grab into my bag. He didn't try to stop me. He never said one word. He just sat there quietly and watched as I left in route to the staircase. Whatever I left behind, I'm sure I could live without, including him. I meant what I said today, every single word, and none of it would be retracted. I'm d-o-n-e-, done! A single tear rolled down my cheek as I made it to the foyer. I didn't bother to look around—that would've been too painful, so I headed for the door ready to leave it all behind until what sounded a lot like a crying baby stopped me. I didn't want to turn around in fear of what I would see, so I stood in place as the cry grew closer. "You're leaving something, Court." Erik was standing right behind me with his phone in his left hand. I took a deep breath, closed my eyes, opened them back, and then turned to him. His face was soaked from tears. His eyes seemed to be swelled shut. He was crying harder than the porcelain baby on the screen, but I didn't let the whimpering phone or my sobbing husband phase me. I'm leaving, and that's that. I didn't look at the baby that now lie frozen on his phone. Instead, I asked, "Who is that?" "That was Katie. I took that video of her the day I was at the agency." He stepped closer to me. "She's coming home soon, Courtney. Please don't leave me here. I need you. Our baby needs you. Don't leave us. Not now. Don't leave our family. I promise Court; I'm going to do better. I'm going to be a good dad and the man you need me to be as Katie's father. I'll step up, just don't leave, Courtney." Damn him! I wanted to yell. I wanted to be angry. I wanted to leave, but suddenly I couldn't move. I couldn't leave my husband or the little girl on his screen that I would soon call my daughter. I don't understand all the equations of my husband, and maybe I never will, but he is my husband. He is the man I married and promised forever to, so I can't leave. Not now and probably not ever. I love this man standing in front of me more than anything else in this world. And my daughter . . . our daughter, I love that much more. I dropped my bags onto the agate flooring. I'm not going anywhere. Erik and I have a family to start.

Chapter Twenty-Nine

KATIE

Two Months Later . . . "Are you sure, Gloria?" "Katie, I'm sure. You're not pregnant." I watched as my physician went over to the sink to freshen up after my appointment was over. "Gloria, what's wrong with me? Eric and I have been trying for two months now, and we're still not pregnant." I've been to my OBGYN more times than I would care to count with her telling me each time I'm still not pregnant. "Katie, it's still too early to tell if there is anything wrong or any specific diagnosis to place on you." "But it's been two months. I've been taking everything from the Clomid you prescribed down to FertilAid. And I cling to that stupid ovulation kit more than I cling to my husband, and I'm still not pregnant. I've done everything, including a few home remedies I read on the internet, so I don't understand." "I don't want you to overexert yourself or stress your body, Katie. I only want you to stick to what I prescribe or recommend. What you read off the internet, or some home remedy is not going to make you become pregnant magically. Sometimes the wait to become pregnant can be more than an anxious couple bargains for, but unfortunately, it can be a part of the process." She dried her hands and threw the paper towel into the small trashcan. "Have you ever thought the issue might be with your husband? We can run a few preliminary tests just to see if the fertility problems lie with him. That could potentially save a lot of time." I caught myself staring into space when I asked, "What if it's not him, Gloria? What if he's fine, and so am I?" I looked at her with what felt like despondency covering my body. "What if there isn't a problem at all? What if we just can't get pregnant?" "Katie, I don't want you to jump to the end of the process before it even starts. This is not the ice age; if there is a reason why you're not getting pregnant, we'll find it. I'll get to the bottom of the issue, if there is one, and then we can go from there." Her words soothed me. "Trust me." She grabbed my hand off my lap. "You're in good hands." "I want this, Gloria . . . I want my baby." "And you and your husband will have your baby soon." I asked, "What about a fertility specialist?" "That is defiantly an option." "And then what?" I was asking questions probably faster than she cared to answer. "If I recommend you to a fertility specialist after . . . ," she emphasized after, "you and . . . ," she emphasized, and "Eric has been through all the fertility tests I administer, the specialist will then get you started on ovulation-inducing drugs. If you're still not pregnant, then we look into IVF. With the In-Vitro process, your egg cells are fertilized by your husband's sperm outside the body. But Katie, IVF is a major treatment in infertility when all other methods of assisted reproductive technology have failed." This cannot be happening. Ovulation inducing drugs . . . In Vitro fertilization . . . What's next? Why can't Eric and I just reproduce the old fashion way? Trust me; we've tried. I don't want to have to go through all of what Gloria is suggesting, but I'll do whatever it takes to give my husband a baby. "Don't worry, Katie. Everything is going to be fine." I trust you, Gloria . . . "Now, before we move any further, I want to get your husband in here." She pulled a small electronic scheduler from her coat pocket. "When can the two of you come back in?" I smiled at Gloria as she scheduled our appointment for her first opening. She handed me a card with the date she scribbled on the font that read the day after tomorrow. "Katie, I'll see you two in here Wednesday morning at nine o'clock." I nodded. "Do you have any questions for me?" "No, I don't think so. I'm just ready to get home and talk to Eric. We'll see you Wednesday morning." This was finally going to happen. Eric and I are going to have our baby. I have the best OBGYN in Baltimore, so I'm confident once she gets Eric in her office, we'll be one step closer. Two Hours Later . . . "Katie, no, I'm not doing it. I'm not going to some damn OGBYN!" were the exact words that shot out of Eric's mouth when I told him about the appointment with Gloria. He flipped out on me, telling me I was dead wrong for making an appointment without talking to him first. He yelled and shouted, not letting me get a word in before he hung up on me. When I called him back to yell and shout at him, his voicemail picked up. An hour later, when he finally called me back—after he apologized for the way he spoke to me—he immediately suggested adoption. Even after I told him we had so many other options left before we even considered adoption, he still heavily suggested that be our next step. He not only suggested adoption, but according to him, he's already contacted an agency and even attended a few meetings to get the process started. I feel ill whenever I think of adopting someone else's baby. In my opinion, that's like going into a stranger's closet and putting on their underwear. I want my own panties and my own baby, damnit! Am I wrong for that? We've experienced a setback, but that doesn't mean we need to run to an adoption agency. Eric and I are two young, vibrant, healthy people. I'm not some over-the-hill hag trying to reproduce, nor am I married to one. According to Gloria, we just need a little more time and a few more tests ran, that's all. We can still have a baby. Eric is the one that said now was the time for us to start a family, so I don't understand why he's acting this way. As I rode home from my yoga class, I sigh as I make a right on President Street. I just want to go home and find Eric there waiting for me, screw his brains out until the sun comes up, pee on a stick, wait for the plus sign, and awaken my sleeping husband to tell him "We're pregnant!" I'll keep my fingers crossed, but I knew that wasn't going to happen. I looked at the navigation screen as my cell phone starts to ring. I looked up at the road then back at the screen. It was Eric. I pressed talk before saying, "Hello." "Hey, Katie, where are you?" "I'm driving home; I went to a yoga class at seven." "That's good, babe. Katie, listen, again, I'm sorry for the way I reacted today. I was out of line." His voice started to perk up when he said, "I saw him today. Katie, I saw our son today." I thought, did I just hear him right? "Did you hear me, Katie? Our counselor, Mrs. Moss, let me see our little boy today." I listened as Eric's cheerful voice came through the Bluetooth. He laughed when he said, "He looks just like you." I didn't find the humor. "He's so tiny, Katie . . . a tiny little chocolate drop. I can't wait until we pick him up!" I huffed through his enthusiasm, "Eric, what are you doing? What are you saying?" I quickly said, "You know it's not too late," before he started back up over some adopted black baby. His voice changed when he asked, "It's not too late for what?" "We don't have to see Gloria, Eric. We don't have to go back to her practice. We don't have to follow up with any of her referrals. We can go someplace else. Somewhere you choose. It's not too late for us to have our own baby. We can keep trying." "Katie, you listen to me, and you listen real good because I'm not repeating the shit. We WILL adopt! I've already taken care of it." "But Eric, it couldn't hurt for both of us to go see a doctor. We should be doing whatever it takes to have our own baby before we consider adopting. I don't want that, especially when there is a chance we can still get pregnant." Eric's voice sent chills through me. "Did you hear a word I just said? We-will-adopt! If you fight me on this, Katie, I'll leave you in that house, and you will never see me again!" Call Ended flashed on the colorful screen. Eric had once again threatened me right before he hung up. Usually, I would burst out into tears, but I think I'm all cried out. My rigid body was numb as I drove down Martin Luther King Boulevard. I just didn't understand this...why was Eric so against us getting pregnant? He's sneaking around to some adoption agency, but why? Why can't my husband just be a normal husband that does normal things like impregnating his wife after he decided it was time for a baby. The call ended close to two minutes ago, but I can still hear his intimidating threats loud and clear: If you fight me on this, Katie, I'll leave you in that house, and you will never see me again! I thought, now what? as I drove the rest of the ride home in silence.

Chapter Thirty

COURTNEY

"Alrighty Shaun, what's next on the checklist?" Shaun and I were working on our first yearly state audit of Fenmore's. I waited as Shaun shifted through the folders scattered in front of him. "Let's see . . . Here we go . . . Insurance claims. We have two claims to assess. One here for Martin Martinez and . . ." He pulled out another sheet of paper. "The second claim is for a Mrs. Katie Morgan-Reynolds." "Okay, let's deal with Martinez first." When Shaun handed me the file, I started to quickly scan everything that was there: He slipped and fell on the icy walk back in December . . . No broken bones . . . No fractures . . . No lawsuits . . . Fenmore's is taking care of all of his medical bills . . . I signed my name on the dotted line as Shaun handed me the next file. I looked at my watch before taking the folder from him. I need this audit business to be over with as quickly as possible so that I could get home to Erik. "This is for that chick that passed out in VIP last summer." I took the file from Shaun and laid it down in front of me before browsing through it. I thought I'm not in the mood for this today. I pinched the bridge of my nose before I looked at the name gawking back at me: Katie Morgan-Reynolds. "Shaun . . ." I sat up closer to the table. "What is it, Courtney?" "Katie Morgan-Reynolds . . . what happened to her again?" I remembered verbatim what Shaun just said, but for some reason, I can't place when the actual incident happened. "You said she was here last summer?" "Yeah, like late summer. She passed out upstairs and was rushed to Mercy Medical Center." Still didn't reregister with me until Shaun said, "You worked with her sister at Citizens." Epiphany! Okay, now I got it. I remember Epiphany being frantic by the time I made it over to them. Soon after, her sister was on a stretcher being rushed out. That's the last I heard of it until now. I start to glance through the file the same as I did the one previous. Nothing caught my eye, so I was all set to sign on the dotted line until I looked at the address on the form: 4882 Montgomery Road, Elkridge, Maryland 21075. Who knew Epiphany's sister and I are practically neighbors? That's funny; Erik and my address is 5769 Landing Road, Elkridge Maryland 21075, which is the next street over. As I swallowed the lump in my throat, I gazed at her last name: Morgan-Reynolds. I then dropped the Morgan and focused only on the Reynolds part. Then my attention flew to her first name: Katie. "Courtney, are you done with that file? We still have to audit all the invoices for the service equipment." I didn't respond to Shaun; I felt as if I was in a stupor unable to. Who was this, Katie Reynolds that made her way to Fenmore's that just so happens to live directly behind my husband and me? "So, with switching out the countertops and cutting boards, it looks like we're twenty thousand dollars over budget from the first quarter." Shaun was into the audit, but I wasn't. I wanted to know more about this, Katie Reynolds. "Shaun, what did she look like?" "Huh?" "Katie Morgan-Reynolds . . . What did she look like? By the time I got to where she was, the paramedics were already taking her out." Shaun smacked his teeth together. "I don't know . . . bleach blonde, slim, big boobs. She looks like she could've had some work done in the past, definitely a tit job. She and Epiphany favor a lot; she's just skinny and a little taller." When Shaun noticed the gravity creeping through my face, he asked, "Byrd, what's wrong?" I couldn't answer him. I was lost inside myself. "Byrd?" Katie? . . . Katie, are you there? . . . Katie! Erik was screaming Katie into his phone the day he dragged me home and strangled me nearly to death. Then there was the night he introduced me to his assistant: "Courtney, this is Katie." "Courtney?" "I'm fine. I'm fine." No, I'm not fine. I'm anything but fine. Every time . . . every single time my husband mentioned Katie started coming into my psyche. "What are you doing? You cannot be serious. We are absolutely not naming our daughter Katie!" "Courtney, please. Katie was my grandmother's name." "Shaun, I'll be back." I jumped up from the table. "Excuse you, where are you going?" "I can't do this right now." "Courtney, the state examiner will be here in the morning." "Shaun, do what you can while you're here. I'll take care of the rest when I get back." The next thing I knew, I was creeping up Montgomery Road with my park lights beaming in the dimming afternoon sun. I had slipped the top half of Katie Morgan-Reynolds' insurance claim information out of Fenmore's with me. I left an incapable events planner to not only man my tapas bar, but also finish our first audit. He had no idea what he was doing there, just like I had no idea what I was doing here, but I couldn't worry about any of that right now—I'm on a mission. I could see the colonial brick modern style home in the distance. I pulled over before I reached my destination. I didn't have to double-check the address on the claim form for Mrs. Katie Morgan-Reynolds; the identical Range Rover parked in the driveway was all the confirmation I needed. I put my Range Rover in park, turned off the engine, and headed to the front door. When I rang the doorbell, there was no answer. I pushed the small lit button again, still without a reply. I thought about trying a third time, but I decided against it. Katie Morgan-Reynolds obviously wasn't home. Why was I here, anyway? What did I want to ask her? What did I come here to see? This was all just one big coincidence. Same last name, same neighborhood, same vehicle. Same license plates. Hers: KRROVER1. Mine: CRROVER1. I'm sure it doesn't mean anything though . . . It's just a coincidence . . . My heart soared to my toes when I heard the front door I was walking away from unlocking. When I went back to the door, I held my breath as this blonde, tanned, blue-eyed, thin white female came into view. I thought this must be her. She asked, "May I help you?" standing in the doorway. "Uh . . . I . . . uh . . ." What do I say? "Sir, may I help you?" I said WHAT DO I SAY Y'ALL? HELP ME! "Sir, what can I do for you?" Quick Courtney, pull it together! "I'm sorry, I'm Courtney Rey . . . Uh-I'm Courtney Byrd. I own Fenmore's down on Canterbury Road." She folded her arms across her perky chest and shot me a look. What was that for? "Yes, Mr. Byrd, what can I do for you?" "I never got an opportunity to extend my apologies to you for your last visit to my establishment. My assistant and I were auditing the year's previous insurance claims when I noticed—" "It was just a panic attack. You don't owe me any apologies." Did she really just cut me off? She did, but I didn't sweat it. I held it together and smiled as I eyed the wedding ring she wore that looked a lot like the one I was wearing on my left ring finger. I didn't sweat that either . . . just another coincidence, right? Please, God, let that be all this is. "Mr. Byrd, if you'll excuse me." She was ready to dismiss me. She already had her hand wrapped around the doorknob ready to push the dark oak door closed. She was done with me, but I wasn't done with her. I needed to make sure she wasn't . . . isn't . . . I don't know what I'm making sure of exactly, but I had to be sure. "Katie . . . Um, Mrs. Reynolds, are you related to Epiphany Morgan?" "She's my sister." "I know her very well. She and I used to work together at Citizens Bank." "Oh yeah, I remember her mentioning you once or . . . Well, once." She didn't seem enthused. "Do you mind if I come in?" I slid the balled-up claim form out of my pocket. "I have an insurance document for you to sign." I lied. "Fine." I'm in! I said, "You have a lovely home," as I walked through the foyer. I was so relieved that nothing in this house matched mine. What was I looking for anyway? When she cleared her throat, I took that as my cue not to go any farther than where I was standing. I guess I wasn't allowed to travel any deeper into her home. I'd seen all I wanted to see anyway, which was nothing. "You said you had some forms for me to sign?" I wanted to say, "Damn bitch, lighten up!" but I kept my mouth shut. "Here you are." I handed her the wrinkled form and my pen. She handed the form back to me after signing it. She then turned on her heels and headed back toward the door. "If we're all finished here . . ." I guess that was another cue for me, and I was happy to oblige. I didn't want to be in her presence any longer than I had to. Goodbye, Mrs. Katie Morgan-Reynolds. Make that bye, bitch! Right before I crossed the threshold to get back to the outside, I looked at the form in my hand. I learned Katie Morgan-Reynolds is Mrs. Dr. Eric Reynolds.

Chapter Thirty-One

KATIE

I hung all the small colorful fish around the babies' new room one after the other. Eric has his heart set on a Finding Nemo theme, so I went with it. Lately, I just follow my husband's lead. I don't question him any more. I don't look at him sideways as I used to when I was trying to figure him out. I just smile and play a good little wife. I don't want to adopt, but I have no other choice. It's what Eric wants, so it has to be what I want, too. We fought every time I protested, so I just stopped. I never made it back to my OBGYN or any other doctor. My husband forbids it and refuses to understand that I want to be a mother so badly but not this way. I stand back and try to admire the baby's nursery. I would like to say it looks good, but I'd be lying. The truth is, the room looks cold and disgusting. It doesn't look like a nursery put together by a mother's love. It really doesn't look like much of anything at all in here other than a page out of a baby catalog. I took a deep breath as the doorbell chimes. It was probably just the

UPS man delivering something I ordered off Amazon that I don't need, so he can just leave it at the door. I thought about sitting in the wooden rocking chair over in the corner of our son's room, but that thought quickly faded. The rocking chair didn't look inviting; it looks even colder than this room does. Maybe I'll feel better when Eric gets home. I always do. Even though my heart is full of resentment toward him and this whole adoption thing, I still love him. As I head down the staircase to see who decided to ring the doorbell a second time, all I could think about was Eric and the new baby. I'm going to call him when I get back upstairs. I know we're going to fight again, but I have to tell him that I cannot go through with this. I don't want to adopt. "Yes, may I help you?" I opened the door without looking out. The guy standing here was definitely not the UPS man. When his words started to jumble, "Sir, may I help you?" shot out of my mouth again. He looked at me like he didn't know what to say. My voice raised an octave when I said, "Sir, what can I do for you?" What the hell was wrong with him, and what did he want? When his urban speech finally came together, he told me who he was and where he was from. Now, what was the owner of that dumpy-ass tapas bar doing here? "Yes, Mr. Byrd, what can I do for you?" I decided to be nice. When he started apologizing for the night I experienced when I was at his restaurant, I cut in with, "It was just a panic attack. You don't owe me any apologies." He should've been apologizing for that awful décor if anything. "Mr. Byrd, if you'll excuse me." I'm done here; we have nothing else to discuss. He stopped me before I could close the door on him. "Katie .

. . Um, Mrs. Reynolds, are you related to Epiphany Morgan?" "She's my sister." "I know her very well. She and I used to work together at Citizens Bank." "Oh yeah, I remember her mentioning you once or . . . Well, once." Is he still here? "Do you mind if I come in?" He slipped something out of his pocket. "I have an insurance document for you to sign." "Fine." Maybe if I sign his little insurance form, he'll go. "You have a lovely home." I cleared my throat, hoping he would catch the hint and leave. This is not a social call. He wasn't invited here, nor was he welcomed here. I don't make it a habit of intertwining with his type. He's a gay black male, so when I say his type since my husband is black, I'm not pulling the race card this time. He's gay! A lot of women say those types of people make terrific friends, but I disagree. All I see when I look at people like him is that three-letter word stamped across their foreheads, and nothing more: G-A-Y. "You said you had some forms for me to sign?" If he would stop looking around my home as if he was seconds away from snatching and running, I could probably have that balled up piece of paper in his hand signed so he could be on his merry little way. I scribbled Mrs. Dr. Eric Reynolds on the form and handed it back to him. "If we're all finished here . . ." We were done, so he could be gone. He looked at the insurance form then back at me. That look in his eyes was all too familiar. I see that same expression whenever my sisters are around. He probably didn't know I was married to a doctor. From that look on his face, he probably instantly became envious of me and the life he imagines that I have. Yep, just like Kyle and Epiphany. He had every right to feel that way. I have a beautiful home; I'm married to a doctor and look at me. Poor thing . . . He'll probably be on Grinder in a few hours praying for some anonymous fling to come over to his dark studio apartment and bend him over. He stood there with his mouth wide open, looking back down to the form. I wanted to tell him Hon get over it. We all can't be married to a doctor, so get your ass back to that over-the-top restaurant and wait for Mr. Whoever and his hard-on.

Chapter Thirty-Two

COURTNEY

I tried with all my strength to keep it together, but I feel like I'm about to lose it right here in the center of this rude bitch living room. My insides were on fire after reading the signature that flashed in front of me. Katie Morgan-Reynolds is Mrs. Dr. Erik Reynolds, and so was I. But that didn't make any sense. I looked at the form before looking back at Katie. My eyes made their way back to the paper in my hand again before they landed on this woman I met only minutes ago. "Is there anything else?" Why is she so nasty? I would slap her across the face if I thought I could get away with it. I quickly shut that thought down, though. I don't look good in stripes, and I despise the colors orange, brown, or faded prison blue. Wait a minute. Wait a minute. Wait-a-minute! Maybe this is just one big coincidence. Katie signed her name Mrs. Dr. Eric Reynolds. E-R-I-C. My husband's name is Dr. Erik Reynolds. E-R-I-K. But . . . He . . . Erik's name is . . . I don't know what to think. I don't know what I'm saying. Hell, I don't even know who I am right now. I also don't know why I came here, but I'm leaving. "Thank you, Mrs. Reynolds. We look forward to seeing you back at Fenmore's very soon." She nodded right before I turned and headed for the door. I'm going back to Fenmore's to finish the audit. No early night for me, just Shaun, blue ink, black coffee, and a lot of paperwork. I turned back to Katie before I stepped out. "Thanks again." When I went to leave, I stopped in my tracks. I faced her. "Where does your husband practice?" Her forehead wrinkled when she asked, "Excuse me?" "Your husband . . . He's a doctor, right?" I'm not going anywhere! I came here for a reason so now is the time for me to stop pretending that I don't know what that reason is because now. . . I do. I thought Erik, what have you done? "My husband's practice is none of your business." Katie turned her nose up toward the ceiling when she answered me. "Is he a dentist?" When she answered, "Yes, my husband is a dentist," I felt as if I had stopped breathing. This situation isn't just a coincidence. This isn't a soap opera. This is my life! Oh, God . . . What is happening? What is going on here? "Look, Mr. Byrd, I am very busy. Thanks again for stopping by." I quickly asked, "Where is your husband right now?" "Why are you asking questions about my husband?" I then asked her, "What does he look like?" She answered me with, "Trust me; you don't know him." "What kind of cologne does he wear?" "Excuse me?" There go those wrinkles in her smooth forehead again. "Where did he sleep last night?" "I'm calling the police!" "He won't be home tonight, will he?" She headed for her phone as my voice raised an octave. "He won't be home tomorrow night or the night after that." She dialed nine-one-one. "He will be back Sunday morning, won't he?" She paused. "And the morning after that, and the morning after that." She slammed her phone face down. "What are you talking about?!" "Who is your husband?" She stood toe to toe with me. "The question is, who the hell are you, and what do you want?" "I'm not Courtney Byrd." "I want you to leave! I'm calling the police department." She left me standing there again. "I'm Courtney Reynolds!" This time she stopped in her tracks without turning back to me. "My last name is Reynolds, just like yours. I have a Range Rover just like yours. I have a home just like yours. I have a ring just like yours. And I have a husband just-like-yours." She turned and ran back over to me. "What are you trying to say?" Her trembles were visible. "Your life . . . Your life is my life—every single part of it." I held the back of my hand out in front of her. "Look at my ring! Canary diamonds just like yours." She didn't look at my left hand that was frozen in her face. "Look at it, damnit! It's just like yours!" "Would you stop saying that! Nothing about you or your life is 'just like mine.' You sound crazy standing there. I have a husband who has a wife—one wife, me! Not you. Not a man, motherfucker! He married a woman, not something like you." "Don't you dare stand there and try to insult me! Bitch, who do you think you are? Or better yet, who do you think I am?" She grabbed her head when she screamed, "Why are you here?! Who sent you? Was it my sisters? My parents?! Who did this? . . . Who sent you here to say these things to me!" She was beyond hysterical. She became panic-stricken right in front of me.

"Answer me, you freak! Answer me! Was it Epiphany? Kyle? That investigator? Was it . . . Was it my . . . Who sent you here? WHO SENT YOU?!" I was crying too, but nothing like her, yet. "Look out your patio." From where we were standing, I could see the top half of my house peeking out through the big, tall pine trees. "That's my home back there, Katie. The home Erik and I share." "Stop it! You don't know my husband . . .You don't know him so shut your mouth! What would Eric want with you? MY HUSBAND IS NOT GAY!" I needed to sit down or at least catch myself before I passed out. I took a step toward the sofa, but my legs wouldn't go any farther. All I could do was pray I didn't faint right in front of this woman. Katie watched my every move. Her eyes dug into my spleen as her silent tears streamed out of her eyes. She hated the words that came out of my mouth. She hated me for being the one that's standing here telling her something she never imagined she'd be hearing. I could tell she wanted me dead. I could tell she wanted to die. And how did I know? Because I wanted to die. I wanted to be released from this nightmare, or at least make-believe none of it is happening. But it's no use. I could pretend all I wanted to, but the fact is . . . my husband has a wife, and her name is Katie. "Just tell me why you're here. Who sent you to me?" "I'm trying to tell you . . . what I'm trying to say is . . . Look, I think your husband is my husband, too." Our heated words restarted. "And I'm telling you that's impossible! Eric is my husband. Do you hear me? My-husband!" "Katie, would you just listen to me." "I've heard enough!" She stopped wailing and looked at me. "My sisters didn't send you here, did they?

You came here on your own. I've seen it all before, though. My husband is a nice man. He's also a nice-looking man, so it's easy for someone like you to be attracted to someone like him. It's also easy for you—" Was she turning her nose up at me? "—to take my husband's kindness and turn it into something else. But what you did today only makes you look bad and confirm my assumptions of you people." Before I could defend myself, she came back with, "You, however, surprise me. Just from looking at you, one would think you were different from those people." Okay, bitch, who are those people? If she would shut up long enough, I could ask her. "You're nice and clean—no visible stubbles. You smell good. You're well versed. You own a restaurant." I thought it's a tapas bar, bitch! "You seem educated. I'm shocked that you would stoop to such a level." "Is that what you think of me? I'm just some gay dude that fell in love with your charming husband's smile one day, followed him home, and decided to tell his wife that I'm not only in love with him, but he and I are also married? How foolish does that sound?" "That's exactly what this is! Why else would you be here if no one sent you?" I shouted out at her, "I'm here because my husband is Dr. Erik Reynolds! I'm not just some sissy nuisance that showed up on your doorstep with some invented story; I'm telling the truth!" "You're cute. I mean, really, really cute." She wasn't crying anymore. "If I was single, and you weren't the way that you are, you and I might actually have a shot." Really? Was she seriously standing in my face mocking me? This couldn't be happening. Erik, who is this woman? Now I was hysterical. "Look, I can prove to you who I am!" "Sure, you can." "Go look at my Range Rover; we have the same SUV with the same licenses-plates! Look . . . I came here because my instincts told me something wasn't right. First, Erik seems to have this infatuation with the name Katie, so when a Katie Reynolds flashed across my desk today, my antennas went up. That's why I came here. I wasn't sure what I would find, but never did I think I would come here to find you." She still didn't believe me. She was looking at me like I was a madman. "Here, Katie . . . I'll prove it to you. I'm not lying!" I flung open the front door, so I could show her my Range that was sitting two houses down. I'll prove it to Ms. High and Mighty exactly who I am. I'll show her that . . . I . . . I . . . I couldn't show Katie anything because my Range Rover was gone. My truck had vanished . . . and so had hers.

Chapter Thirty-Three

KATIE

My heart was pounding. My pulse was racing. My mind was on maximum overload. I screamed. I cried, I shot dirty looks, but none of it stopped him from saying these things to me. He was right; I wanted to die . . . I wanted to die and take him with me, so he would stop claiming he has some sort of relationship with my husband. The things he was saying to me . . . the allegations of a marriage? With Eric? Where did that even come from? Who orchestrated this? I had to know before I exploded in my skin, but he wouldn't give me the satisfaction of telling me what I needed to hear. He just kept going on and on about him and my husband. He wouldn't stop—it seems as if he would never stop. He brought up one claim after the other to help support his bullshit. At this point, I just need to reach Eric. I need him to come home and get me away from this person since he won't leave. I'm under enough stress without having to deal with this ridiculous, sissy punk. Once this is all over, we're moving out of this house, out of this city, out of this state! I wanted to be far away from a place where some random stranger would show up on a wife's doorstep and make such claims. I don't know what to think as this person stands here, claiming he is married to my husband. How absurd is that? Eric is my husband! I wanted to laugh, but I couldn't stop crying long enough. Maybe I don't know everything there is to know about Eric, but I do know he's not gay. If he was, why would he want me? What could I do for a man that wants a man? Absolutely nothing! Even if Eric wanted a man, which he doesn't, he wouldn't want Courtney Byrd. Eric would never date inside his race. He told me so. He said he wasn't attracted to black women, so I'm pretty sure that goes for black men, too. I just wanted to know what would make this creature come here and say these things to me? If no one sent him here, then why was he here? Why did he pick my door? Why did he pick my husband? I had nothing. No answers, just this . . . this man standing here trying to convince me of something that just wasn't true. The good news is I wasn't falling for any of it, and I refuse to amuse this stalker any longer. I sniffled as the last tear rolled down my face. The words that I allowed to fill my ear gates simply were not factual, and I've had enough. I didn't want to cry anymore; I wasn't even furious at this Courtney person standing inches away from me any longer. Being the wife of someone like my husband, this kind of irritation was bound to happen sooner than later. I didn't think it would be taken quite this far, though. Eric is a gorgeous man. He's a wealthy dentist in a big city. He's well-known. He's affluent. He's sexy. He's everything any woman—and apparently some men—would want, so of course, they're going to be a few strays that follow him home, white or black, and obviously, male or female. "I've heard enough!" I was done with this conversation. We had nothing more to discuss. It amazes me that I've entertained him this long. I didn't have to hear anymore because I already knew Courtney's real story, and I told him so; seconds after I figured him out. He seemed offended as I read him like a book. I didn't care. It was his own fault. How dare he come into my home and say these things to me? He deserved what I was giving him, and then some. I attacked his character along with his sexuality. I threw blow after blow toward him. I even tossed in a few you people just for effect. I hear gays hate that with a passion, so I'll say it a few more dozen times just to piss him off even more. I'll make his filthy black-ass pay for coming here today, and once my husband finds out exactly who Courtney Byrd is, he'll pick up where I left off. Now he was screaming and throwing his arms in the air, probably doped up on opioids and weed. That wouldn't be out of the norm for those people. Now I am pulling the race card. "Here, Katie . . . I'll prove it to you. I'm not lying!" As he headed to the door shouting something about licenses-plates, I headed for the phone. I wasn't calling the police department . . . uh-huh . . . I'm calling Eric. He needs to come home right now! As I held my phone in my hand, ready to dial my husband's number, it started to ring. The caller ID indicated it was Eric calling, so I immediately pressed talk. "Eric, honey, where are you?" I could hardly make out what his low-toned voice was saying under all the static on the line. "Eric . . . can you hear me?" We suffered a lousy connection. "Eric? Honey, are you there?" I spoke loud enough for Courtney to hear me. "Eric, we have a bad connection." Suddenly, the static stopped. The line was now crystal clear. I could hear my husband perfectly. "Eric, you need to come home right now. We have a big problem." "Meet me at home." That was Eric's deep voice humming on the other end of the phone. "Meet you at home?" I'm confused. I'm at home. "Meet me at my other home—Courtney will lead the way." "Eric, what-what are you talking about? Courtney will lead the way where?" I turned and looked at Courtney standing near the door with his cell phone in his hand. He wasn't shouting anymore; his arms lie calmly down by his sides. He was looking at me as if he was waiting for my call to end. I didn't have to ask him who the caller was on his phone that caused his skin to turn pale beige. I knew it was Eric because Courtney's expression was just . . . like . . . mine.

Chapter Thirty-Four

DR. REYNOLDS

I sat quietly in mine and Courtney's immaculate eat-in kitchen as I waited for my wives to come through the door in a single file. I'm sure Courtney would be first, with Katie right behind. Courtney must be first. Courtney then Katie—that's how I planned it. If Courtney doesn't walk through that door first, my design is ruined! It would all go up in smoke. I must see Courtney's eyes first, then Katie's. At the beginning of our three-way union, Katie was always first since she came into my life one hundred seventy-two hours before Courtney did. Now, here at the end, the tables must be reversed. I've walked through this scene four thousand five hundred, twenty-six times in my head. I've reenacted it three thousand, four hundred fifty times aloud. Everything must be just right or, as my wives would say, everything has to be perfect. I already knew what I was going to say once Courtney and Katie got here. I knew how I was going to sit. I knew how my posture should be, and I also knew exactly when to pull the trigger.

But that would be later. First, we would have twenty-two minutes of conversation, which will give both of my wives' eleven minutes of alone time with me. During and after their Q and A sessions, I would allow seven hundred twenty-one tears to fall out of my eyes accompanied by thirty-one sniffles. The clock read four ten. I told Courtney not to walk in this house a minute before four fourteen. I will start speaking right at four fifteen. If either of them comes here a second sooner, I'll kill them both. I hope Courtney and Katie follow my instructions because I don't want to hurt either of them more than I already have. I love my wives. I didn't want to bring any harm to them, but unfortunately, someone is going to die today. At precisely four thirty-seven, a heart will stop, blood will start, and tears will pour. My double life was about to end. It will all be over before the clock strikes five, but for now, I am still Erick, E-R-I-C-K Reynolds. A little play on spelling, but my name really is Erick Reynolds. However, I'm not a dentist. I never attended med school. I never even finished high school. I dropped out in the tenth grade to take care of my dying father. He became bedridden from lung cancer and was unable to care for himself or me any longer, so I had to work to support both of us. I don't have any other family; I never knew my mother or any of her relatives. It was just my father and me. Ten years ago, my father died in a ratty old shack out in the middle of nowhere that we used to call home. He left this earth with six dollars, seventy-two cents in his pocket. I counted it the day he died. I still have that six dollars, seventy-two cents. I count it every hour on the hour. I start by examining the five-dollar bill. FEDERAL

RESERVE NOTE rested right above Abraham Lincoln's head. To the left of the dead president is the serial numbers that I have memorized: ID40784297A. To the right of ol' Abe reads THE UNITED STATES OF AMERICA. I know every piece of that five-dollar bill from my daddy's pocket. Same for the one-dollar bill, the two quarters, the two dimes, and the two pennies. I have to study real hard to keep things in my brain. When I was in school, teachers always told me I was different and needed special attention because I wasn't like the other children, but my dad never paid them any mind. He just said I was lazy right before he stumped me into the ground for having my teachers disturb him. In-between his punishments, he told me I might as well drop out of school because I wouldn't amount to anything anyway. He also said he wasn't worried about me becoming a drug dealer or gangbanger because I didn't have enough sense to do either. He said I'll probably die in some mental institution due to my screwed-up brain cells. Well, he was wrong. I didn't die in some institution; I'm living my life on the outside. He was wrong about me . . . they were all wrong about me. I looked up at the clock when I heard the front door creak open. It was four fourteen and twelve seconds . . . Courtney and Katie were right on time. "I'm in here." I didn't raise my voice. They'll find me. "Erik?" It was Courtney; he came toward me eight seconds before Katie did. They were such good wives. They obeyed my every command. They both loved me to pieces. They worshipped me. I just hope they can live without me . . . "Eric, what are you doing here?" Poor Katie; what I'm about to tell her will probably destroy her for good. She wasn't strong like Courtney. She was clingy, more emotion-driven, whereas Courtney was the independent wife. He wanted me right by his side just as much as Katie did, if not more, but he could hold his own while I was away. That's what I loved most about him. I also loved the way Katie's face would glow whenever I came through the front door carrying my black leather briefcase full of newspapers and a blanket that I passed off as paperwork from my upscale practice in Potomac that never existed. Courtney and Katie are both so different but so much alike, which is exactly why I picked them to spend my time on earth with. I'm going to miss both of them so very much. "Erik, say something." "Courtney, where do you want me to start?" "Eric, you can start by telling me what the hell is going on!" "Katie, please don't yell. This isn't the time." "You better start talking, right now!" "Katie, if I have to tell you again to lower your voice, you will regret it." "Erik, what's going on here?" That's more like it, Courtney. Nice and calm. Obey. I didn't waste any more time. I had rehearsed this moment, so I was prepared. Here goes. "Courtney, Katie, I'm married . . . to both of you." They both shrieked, "What!" in unison. "I said, I married both of you." "Wait a minute, hold-on! Eric, you better start explaining yourself right now!" I looked at Katie first. "Katie, after my father passed away, I swore I wouldn't end up like him. I wasn't going to die alone and lonely without anyone to call my own. I made a vow to myself that I would find the right one for me. So, I started searching. I searched for nine and a half years to find just the right woman. She had to look a certain way. She had to dress a certain way. She had to act a certain way. She had to fit the mold that had created in my head." "The mold?" Katie seemed almost frightened to ask. "Yes, Katie. The mold of how I always envisioned my mother would be. I never met her until the day I saw you at the library. It was you, Kate. You were the one I was looking for. I used to dream of you every night before we even met. I would paint your image on the walls in my father's house twice per day after he died: once in the early morning, and again before the sunset. I had to meet this woman that was camped out in my brain. I had to bring her into reality. I wanted to bring you out of my dreams, Katie." I closed my eyes. "I can still remember your straight blonde hair, your blue eyes, and your petite body. Your beauty . . . It was you, Katie. The woman in my head . . . the picture-perfect woman in my dreams was not my mother, it was you, so I had to find you so I could have you. I kept drawing you on my walls so I wouldn't forget you. I had to have a constant reminder of you. When I saw you in the flesh at the library that day, I knew you were that woman, Katie. You were the wife I married two hundred eighty-six thousand, four hundred and fifty times over in my head. Now all I had to do was make you my wife." "Erik, what are you saying? None of that makes any sense!" Now it was Courtney's turn. "My precious Courtney, when I first saw you in the supermarket, you reminded so much of my dad when I was a little kid. He wasn't always a monster; he used to be kind to me like a father was supposed to be. He was very handsome like you, Courtney. Smart too until he got sick. When we talked outside the store, even the tone of your voice reminded me of my father, so I couldn't let you go.

I didn't want to lose my daddy again, so I gave myself to you because I knew if you had me, you would never leave me. I'm not gay, Court. I've never even looked at another man in a sexual or relationship way before, but the only way I could have all of you is by giving you all of me. It's like . . . when I looked at you standing there, all I could see was love and devotion from a person that I didn't even know. You were a stranger, but you seemed so familiar to me. You were my father all over again. I didn't want to be married to a husband, so I married you and made you my wife." Courtney and Katie both looked at me like I had just sprouted two heads. "Erik, I don't understand any of that. Katie is not your mother, and I am not your father. You had no right to mold us into what you needed us to be. I wanted you to love me because of the person I am, not because of who you imagined me to be. That's sick, Erik! YOU are sick!" "So . . . what the investigator found on you . . . it was true." Tears started streaming out of Katie's eyes. "My sisters tried to show me, but I didn't want to listen because I didn't believe it. I ripped it up because it wasn't true! I never saw signs of any illnesses, especially not schizophrenia . . . until now. You are a sick sociopath that should be locked away, not out destroying lives!" "You're right, Katie. That's all I am is a sick man. I'm not this rich, powerful dentist you and your sisters thought I was. I was homeless before I married the two of you. When the city condemned my father's house, I was living on the streets until I decided to rest my head in a rescue shelter." "Erik, stop it! Stop all of this right now! I don't believe you! None of this is true, and you know it! You are a liar!" "Courtney, everything I'm saying right now is the truth." "No-it's-not! You are a doctor. I met your hygienist the night you brought her and your brother to Fenmore's!" Katie shot a look over to Courtney, probably realizing she met that same set of imposters. "The woman you met that night Courtney, her name is Amy. She isn't a hygienist; she's homeless just like I was. She, her husband Thaddeus, and their daughter Miranda are all homeless. They played a friendly little game of dress up for the three crisp fifty-dollar bills I promised." "Erik, why? That's all I want to know is why?" I peered over at Courtney. "I heard Shaun talking about me. 'Where is his family?' 'Where are his friends?' Why haven't you met any extensions of him?' Well, guess what? I had a family that night. A friend too. That's why I did it. I wanted to prove myself to both of you at the same time, in the same way, in the same place." "My god, Erik, stop! Why are you talking this way? I've never seen this side of you before." "Courtney, that's because you never knew the real me. Neither of you did. I kept him hidden so I could love you the way you wanted to be loved. I couldn't do that as the man that's sitting here right now, so I created a man that could." "ERIK, STOP IT! You're full of shit! How does a homeless man go from living in a shelter to having two different million-dollar lifestyles? Answer that! All the lavished shit. The freakin' good life, Erik! Jamaica, the Range Rovers, my tapas bar. How did you do it all? If what you're saying is true, how did you do it? HOW DID YOU DO IT?!" Courtney was furious, and it showed. I've never seen his light almond complexion turn this shade of red before, but I had to keep going. "Court, I grew up dirt poor. Most nights, we had no food—some winters, we had no heat. Me and my dad lived in horrible conditions. My father had nothing but a twenty-million-dollar life insurance policy. On his death bed, he told me he struggled and paid the premium every month since the day I was born. His last words to me were, 'I would rather you be a rich dummy than a poor one.' He loved me just enough to hand me a twenty-million-dollar cushion to soften the blows he knew life would deal someone like me. I used his money for good. I didn't touch a penny of it until I met the two of you." "You claimed you love me . . . how could you hurt me this way?" "I do love you, Katie. We were going to start a family together." "Oh yeah?" She looked at Courtney. "And what were you going to do with him?" "I was going to start a family with him, too." "So, is he the reason you didn't want to go to my OBGYN? Is he where all that adoption nonsense came from?" "Katie, I didn't have to go see a doctor." "Why not?!" Now Katie's skin tone changed color. "Because I had a vasectomy thirteen years ago. I would never risk genetically passing on my illness to a child. I couldn't reproduce with you or anyone else even if I wanted to." Katie shouted, "You what?!" right before her left hand landed across my cheek. She had every right to assault me. They both did. I destroyed a portion of their lives they will never get back. Right now, I'm the bad guy in this story even though my intentions were good. I tried to be a perfect husband to them both, providing them the kind of lives most people only dream of. I catered to them. Anything they wanted was theirs, including the illusion of a dream man. If I'm guilty of anything, it would be allowing myself to be loved by both my wives. Katie's watery eyes looked over at Courtney then back at me. "So that's where the babies name came from . . . You went and picked out a little black baby boy to name him Courtney." Courtney shrieked, "Whoa! Our white baby girl was going to be named Katie!" "That's right," I confirmed. Remember . . . I'm not holding anything back. "So, what about Epiphany?" I looked at Courtney. I asked, "What about her?" "You knew she worked with me at Citizens, didn't you?" "I did." "That day at the bank . . . I was going to introduce you to her . . . you were sitting right in my office . . . right there at my desk. I was going to introduce you as my husband, but I didn't get a chance to because you left. Now I know why . . . She couldn't see you sitting there, could she . . . not as my husband anyway, because you're her sister's husband!" "Court, I—" "Don't you DARE 'Court' me! That is so . . . Oh, my God, you are a monster, Erik! You are a sick monster to play such reckless games with people!" "I didn't know at first, Court . . . but once I found out you and Epiphany worked together, I went and bought the lease to the building you wanted and got you out of there ASAP." I could tell Katie was trying to hold it together, but she was losing the battle quickly. "I don't know who you are. I don't know if you're Eric Reynolds, Erik Reynolds, Erick Reynolds, Dr. Reynolds . . . I don't know what you've done to me, nor do I understand why you did it, but I'm out of here! I can't stand to look at you for another second!" I jumped out of the chair and shouted, "Katie, wait! I'm Erick Reynolds. I switched up the spelling of my first name so I could maneuver and manipulate any and everything I needed to without so many questions. Deeds, contracts, receipts." I paused for a quick second. "Marriage licenses. I had to be one man with you, Katie, so that I could be another man for Courtney." "Ugh, Eric, that is disgusting! You fucking sick nasty bastard, I'm leaving." "Don't leave. This isn't over!" "The hell it's not!" "You promised me, Katie . . . You said you would never leave me. You said you wouldn't walk out on me. That's what you told me. I remember the words that came out of your mouth. You said, 'I promise.' Did you think I would forget? Do you think I'm dumb or something? Like I can't remember things. I remember everything, Katie! EVERYTHING! I'm not stupid. I'm not some nut job that can't remember a promise!" I was screaming into cold silence. Katie and Courtney just looked at me. I couldn't tell what they were thinking, and I probably didn't want to know. I just wanted to be heard. I wanted to be understood. I wanted them to know why I did what I did. I tried explaining myself, hoping that would be enough, but it wasn't nearly enough. They wanted more. They asked for the truth even though that's just what I was giving. Instead of embracing me so we could possibly move on with our lives, they looked at me with contempt. They both started to stare at me like I was insane. But they have to know that I'm not crazy. I'm not that slow kid my teachers told my dad I was, and I'm for surely none of the things my father led me to think I was. If only we had more time, I could explain more. I wanted to tell them that I am schizophrenic, but I take my meds. They didn't have to be afraid of me. I'm not a psychopath. Psycho and schizo are totally different. At least to me, they are. I can't help who I am or how I came out; all I can do is calculate every aspect of my life all the way down to the second to make sure I don't mess up. So you see, I'm not a bad guy; I just want to be heard but time's up . . . That's all folks . . . "Erik!" "Oh my God, Eric, what are you doing?!" Katie didn't look as if she wanted to leave anymore; when she saw the revolver resting right above my right temple, her tune quickly changed. "Eric, what are you going to do with that gun?" I could see her heart beating through her silk blouse. Her fear matched Courtney's horror. "Erik, put the gun down!" He didn't want me to kill myself, and neither did Katie. They wanted me to stay on this earth living in shame for what I've done to them. For a split second, I changed my mind. I no longer wanted to kill myself like I originally planned, but I can't stay here on this earth being considered something that I wasn't. I'm not an evil man. I'm not cruel. I'm not a cheater. I love my wives, and I proved it. I'm an honest man with a good heart, but they don't see me like that anymore, so I have to go. Courtney and Katie both were prepared to break their promises and leave me. They were ready to vanish from my life without so much as a random thought for my well-being. They would've had me put away. I would've died in some intuition just like my father said I would. But the jokes on them . . . "Erik, you can't—" "Eric, no please—" "No, Erik, no—" "God, no! Eric, just listen—" "NO, ERIK, WAIT! . . . ." The room was filled with pleads for me to lower the gun from my head, but that wasn't going to happen. I tuned my wives out as my eyes watched the clock. It was seconds away from the time I planned to die. "Erik, listen to me."

Courtney was crying so hard I no longer recognized his face. "I won't leave you. I don't understand any of this, I don't know what you've done or how you did it with Katie and me, but I do know that I love you with all my heart. That hasn't changed. You asked me not to leave you; now I'm begging you not to leave me. Erik don't do this! Don't leave what we've built. We have a child to raise. We have a life to live—just me and you. I'll stand by you through all of this. We can pick up right where we left off, just don't go. I won't be able to survive behind it. Don't, Erik, please. Please!" It wasn't enough. Courtney's desperate plea and Katie's silent implore wasn't enough to keep me in this world. They both made a promise to stay with me, but, just like I knew they would, they both were ready to bail on me today. So, I'm taking off before they have a chance to. My mother walked out on me and, in a way, so did my father. I couldn't take Katie or Courtney doing the same, so I had to end it now. One-half second after the wall clock read four thirty-seven, I couldn't hear anything anymore. No more pleas, no more questions, no more sobs. The kitchen grew silent. I see Courtney's mouth still moving, but I couldn't make out a single word he was saying. His words and Katie's face were all a blur. The bullet I just put in my skull made everything fuzzy. It stung like hell at first, but the pain was fading. Now my legs started to feel weak. I couldn't support myself anymore. Now my vision went completely black. I could feel my heart rate slowing way down, too. I couldn't breathe anymore. It was over. I was dying second by second. I was fading into the darkness that surrounded me. I would tell my wives just how much

I love them one last time, but I was gone. My last breath had already escaped me. I had killed myself right in front of them, and there was no coming back. They were good to me . . . We were good together. I lived a full, rich life with both Katie and Courtney; too bad it's all over now. My time has come and gone. As they scurry around the kitchen over my dead body, I trust Katie and Courtney will find it in their hearts to forgive me and try and move on with their lives, even though I knew they never would do either. They would suffer dearly for what I've done to them, and I would pay on the other side for ruining three lives: Katie's, Courtney's, and . . . my own. Well, goodbye, my loves . . . Goodbye.

Chapter Thirty-Five

KATIE

"Katie! Oh, Katie, are you okay?" "What's wrong, sweetie?" You guessed it; it's my sisters. Kyle and Epiphany charged toward me as soon as the north elevator doors opened. They came to the hospital minutes after I called them. All I said to Epiphany when she answered her cell was, "Meet me at Mercy Medical Center as soon as you can." Twenty minutes later, she and Kyle were here. They had no idea why I was at the hospital or why I needed them here with me. That would soon change. They didn't know any of Eric's secrets or the fact that he killed himself and was lying in the cold, drafty morgue wearing nothing but a toe tag. I planned to tell Kyle and Epiphany everything once they settled down. As bad as I want to sit here with love still in my heart for the man I knew as Eric Reynolds, there was nothing left inside of me. He wasn't my husband. He wasn't the man of my dreams. He wasn't a man at all. He was a coward! He didn't even have the common courtesy to stick around and face the mess he made of innocent lives. Instead, he played the victim and ran for the hills with his penis tucked between his legs and a revolver in his lap. I hope that sick bastard rots in hell for what he's done. I didn't ask for someone like Eric, nor did I deserve to be in the position he put me in. He led me to believe the world he gave me was reserved just for me; never once did he mention I would be part of a cast. "Katie, please just tell us what's going on." "Kyle . . . Epiphany . . ." I braced myself. "Eric is dead." I then relaxed as my sisters went crazy. They didn't know the story behind my husband's death; all they heard leave my lips was, 'Eric is dead,' and probably assumed his death was right up there with a family tragedy. Eric killing himself was far from a tragedy even though my sisters were crying hysterically. They had no idea what that twisted bastard did to me. As Kyle and Epiphany shed tears for Eric, I sat emotionless. He's gone, and that was just that. My numb heart wouldn't allow me to morn. "Katie, what happened? Are you okay?" "I'm fine." Sniffles. "What happened to Eric?" "He killed himself." Kyle jumped out of her seat next to me. "He did what!" My unruffled face looked up at her as I repeated myself. "He killed himself." "God, Katie, no!" Epiphany asked, "Where? Uh, where did this happen?" "In his home," I answered without hesitation. I had nothing to hide. I promised myself I would unleash everything to my sisters, and I was doing just that. Kyle sat back down. "He killed himself at home? Were you there?" "I was there. I watched him do it. I stood there as he put a gun to his head and pulled the trigger . . . We both watched." "Both? Who else was there?" I looked at my little sister when

I answered, "Courtney." "The hygienist was there?" "No, no, Epiphany. Eric didn't have a hygienist named Courtney." Epiphany dabbed tears from her eyes when she said, "You're losing me." "Eric didn't have a practice in Potomac; he wasn't a traveling dentist; he wasn't a doctor at all." "Well, who was that woman we met that night at Fenmore's?" I wanted to choke up blood the second I heard the name Fenmore's fill the air. It was hard, but I was about to expose Eric and all of his dirty laundry. My sisters had a right to know who this man really was since I obviously didn't. I spoke as Kyle and Epiphany listened closely. Their eyes widen, their teeth gritted, and I think I even heard Kyle release a few choice cuss words that I wouldn't dare repeat. They were listening to my life's story in awes. And I don't blame them. This kind of thing didn't happen every day. This isn't a typical situation, which is why my sisters sat on the edge of their seats in disbelief. Their faces read they wanted to hear more, but I'm not sure how much more they could take. And to be honest, I'm not sure how much more I could take. It stung to speak of Eric and his male bride. It hurt me to my core to think everything he was saying and doing to me was being said and done to the other wo-man in his life. And it kills me that Eric left me here to deal with his mess. I still have questions that demand answers. I have angered tears that needed to be wiped away. I have a broken heart that required mending. I needed Eric to look me in my eyes and tell me why he did this to me. Why me? . . . Why did he choose me? I'm not his fucking mother, so why couldn't he have chosen the next blonde that walked by? I hated what I was admitting to my sisters, but it all had to be told. I will no longer walk around, faking a perfect life with an Hermès bag swinging from my forearm, and my nose pointed toward heaven. Let's face it; I'm not the wife of a doctor any longer. My title isn't Mrs. Dr. Eric Reynolds anymore. Eric saw to it that I was stripped of my life, my home, my dignity, and his name. I wouldn't try to hide any of that from Kyle or Epiphany; I was prepared to tell my story to a stranger if he asked. The secrets my husband kept would no longer be hidden. I would expose him and his concealed life to the galaxy if I could. Once my admission became unsealed from behind my quivering lips, my sisters' questions started flying so fast, I felt myself becoming queasy. "He was married to Courtney Byrd?! Are you talking about my Courtney?" I thought I wouldn't necessarily call him your Courtney, Epiphany. "Courtney? The guy that worked with Epiphany at Citizens?" "How could he marry Courtney?" "Was Eric gay?" "Is Courtney gay?" "Was the marriage legal?" "Where did they live?" "Will the marriage be annulled?" "Will you still be considered his widow?" "Is Courtney still considered his wife?" "Eric wasn't a doctor?" "Which shelter was he at?" "How long was he there?" "Where did he live before?" "If he wasn't a doctor, how did he support the three of you?" "He opened that restaurant for Courtney?" "He was prepared to put you through law school?" "Why didn't he just tell you he had a vasectomy?" "Why was your Range Rover black and Courtney's was white?" "Where did the trucks disappear to?" "Did he take them?" "Why did Eric bring you to Fenmore's that night?" "Why didn't you tell us you sliced your hand opened after you left the hospital?" "Was Eric gay?" I would swear to it that question was already asked. As my sisters' loud voices filled the entire wing of the hospital, I got up and excused myself after I assured them I was okay. I told them I needed to go to the ladies' room and promised I'd be right back. Before I answered any more questions, I had to get away. I wouldn't be gone long; I just needed a little time alone. As I left the area, I could tell they were watching me. Epiphany even looked as if she was a breath away from asking for my belt and shoelaces. That wouldn't be necessary, though. The pain I feel in the pit of my stomach for what Erick has done to me is worse than unbearable, but I'm committed to getting through this. I won't let Erick Reynolds have any more control over me. He is out of my life for good, and I just have to accept that. On my trip back from the lavatory, I saw the man that shared his life with my husband sitting in a different family waiting room. He was only a few feet away from me, yet we seemed miles apart. I wanted to go over and say something to him. Maybe we should talk; console each other since we are the only two people on earth that know the suffocating pain that man left behind. I decided to keep my distance, though. I never wanted to see Courtney Byrd again. Not because I disliked his kind, as I stated a few chapters ago. I just didn't want to face him. He would be a constant reminder of what I was going through and why. I just couldn't put myself through that a thousand times over, so in that case, I would make sure Courtney Byrd and Katie Morgan's paths never shall cross again. I'll disappear and bury myself in the quarry of his life until maybe one day, I'm less than a distant memory inside of him. That's the way I wanted it, and that's how it was going to be. I tried not to stare at him sitting there, but I couldn't help it. He was crying violently. He looked as if he would never stop. I would go over and tell him everything would be okay, but I wasn't sure it would be. I'm committed to getting through this, but I still had to wonder if I ever will. I turned and headed back to my sisters. Suddenly, I didn't want to be apart from them. I needed them and was grateful they were here. I bid Courtney a distant, silent farewell as I walked away, sharing the hell we were placed in by our husband.

Chapter Thirty-Six

COURTNEY

I begged him not to go. I looked into his eyes and pleaded with him to stay with me. I would have listened to him. I would've made myself understand his reasons why. I would have done whatever it took to make Erik stay, but I guess nothing I said or did was enough because he's dead. He left me with nothing but his scent, my tears, and random suicide thoughts of my own. If Shaun weren't sitting beside me, holding my hand for what feels like dear life, I would slip into the men's restroom and end it all. I hated myself for these reckless notions, but I can't help it. How was I supposed to survive without my husband? How was I supposed to process this and just move on? Erik has been gone just a few hours, and his death has already consumed me, and I . . . I don't want to get better. I don't want to get over this. I want to die! I want to leave this planet just like he did. Maybe I'll meet him in the sky. We could fall in love all over again without his other wife invading our time. That bitch, I wanted to spit just thinking about Katie. She is the one to blame for all of this. When she said she was leaving him, that's when he jumped up and pulled out that gun. She needs to go downtown to the Baltimore Police Department and turn herself in for murder because she killed my husband! "Byrd, are you okay?" Shaun was right by my side. I didn't know who else to call, so I called him. I'm sure Mama would've come too, but I didn't want to see her right now. Actually, I didn't want to see Shaun anymore either. I just want to be left alone. Shaun stood up beside me. "Courtney, let's go grab a soda." "I don't want anything." My shaking voice was so low I'd be shocked if Shaun made out what I just said. "Well, would you like some water?" "Shaun, I don't want anything, all right. I'm fine!" "Okay well . . ." He sat back down. "I'm not going anywhere." "I thought you were going to get something to drink?" "No, we were going to get something to drink. Courtney, I'm not leaving you like this." "Shaun . . ." I broke down crying. I couldn't sensor my insides any longer. I was beyond frantic. I was so deep in pain, I became unhinged. How could he leave me? He told me he loved me. He said he cared about me. We lived as husband and wife. We were husband and wife! Fuck Katie! That pale bitch didn't know him as I did. She couldn't make him laugh the way I did. She couldn't hold him in the middle of the night like I could. It was me he loved. I was his wife. Fuck that bitch! FUCK HER! I want her dead for what she stole from me. She didn't love Erik; I did! I was the good wife. I was the one he came home to. IT WAS ME, NOT

HER! "Courtney, get up!" Shaun wrestled with my rigid body after I landed in the middle of the floor in a fit of rage. "Courtney, please get up." I didn't want to leave this spot. At least not until my husband did. I want to leave Mercy Medical Center at the same time as Erik—be transferred to a funeral home just as he was going to be. We could go at the same time; be together again. I would go through the transformation from life to death with the hopes of seeing Erik again. I just needed to touch him. Tell him how much I love him. I wanted to live in the same space as he did, even if it was in the depths of hell. I would spend eternity laced with unquenchable fire if it meant being with my husband. "I'm going to get a nurse!" Shaun shouted as he ran off. "No! Don't . . . Don't do that. I'm okay. Really . . . I'm fine." I didn't want some nurse coming in here to administer something that was supposed to calm me down. I didn't want to calm down. I didn't want to relax. I didn't want to breathe easier. I didn't want to breathe at all. I didn't want anything except the man I married. That's it . . . I wouldn't allow anything else to soothe me from this point on. "Here you are, sir." The nurse's aide handed Shaun two clear cups with what looked like water inside. My screams must've been heard a second ago, and the aide was ordered to bring me this little-ass cup of water as if it would make everything all better. Well, it won't make anything better, but I'll try to calm down for Shaun's sake. I have to make him think I'm okay long enough to get away from him. "Are you ready to tell me what happened?" asked Shaun taking a sip from his cup. I'm not telling him anything. He knew Erik was dead, but that was it, and we were going to keep it that way. No one would ever know the real story. I would take it to my grave. I would never even repeat any of it to myself in fear that I would betray me and release the intimate details of his death. Erik is gone . . . That's all the world needed to know. The details would never be disclosed. "I don't want to talk about it right now, Shaun, okay." "He didn't try to hurt you, did he?" Hurt me? Why would he ask if Erik tried to hurt me as if he knew Erik hurt himself? That's not what happened. At least, that's not the way I'm going to tell it. I didn't know which rendition I would provide for inquiring minds, but Erik placing a gun to his head and pulling the trigger would surely be left out. "My husband would never hurt me. What would make you even ask such a thing?" "I'm sorry. I just want to know what happened." "Are details that important right now, Shaun? The fact is Erik is gone! Okay, gone! He's not coming back next week, next month, or ever! My husband is dead! Do you hear me, Shaun? He's gone, and I can't change that!" "Okay, Courtney, calm down. I don't want to upset you." Shaun tried to speak as carefully as he could. He claims he didn't want to upset me, but it was too late for that. Why did he want to know what happened to Erik anyway? Probably, so he could go spread the news to every queen he could reach via text message. Well, I wasn't having that. I'll kill Shaun and take half of those queers with me first. My crying spell was subsiding. My insides were contained for now. I'll hide what I really feel until I get to the parking garage. There were so many paramedics in the ambulance with Erik, we couldn't ride to the hospital with him. Katie drove to the hospital as I raced one hundred miles per hour behind her. Erik had stashed both of our trucks in our garage after he confiscated them from the home he shared with Katie. Why did he do it? I'll never know, and I don't care. That isn't important now. Nothing is important anymore. The parking garage . . . I'll end it all in the parking garage. I won't live without him. I won't allow myself to exist any further without my other half. Erik made this bed . . . now I was about to lie in it. I started crying again as I thought about the life I once owned. I was so happy with Erik. I had a flourishing new business, a beautiful home, nice things, and, most importantly, a man whom I loved, and he loved me. I can still hear his keys jingling in the locks back at home. When he would turn his key and unlock our front door, I swear that door key held the lock to my soul because I felt set free when he entered our home. I was set free from the black hole painted in my life led by his absences. When he would come home, I could breathe again as his cologne breezed through the air. My life always restarted when he came home. When he wasn't there, I felt like a drugless dope fiend yearning for another hit. All I want is my husband. I don't care about anything else. Heaven and earth can pass away right now, as long as I have Erik, I'll be okay. I know it's wrong and unnatural to feel this way, but I can't help it. I can't control it, and if I could, I wouldn't. "Courtney . . ." Shaun bumped me back into reality. "What is it, Shaun?" "Do you know her?" I looked up to see Katie Morgan looking in on me. She didn't move; it seems as if her shiny stilettos were glued to the floor. She didn't say anything to me; she didn't come any closer. She just stood there right in front of the elevators and stared at me. I wonder what's going through her head right now. What is she thinking? Guess I'll never know that either . . . "Courtney, who is she? She looks so familiar." I looked Katie dead in the eyes from afar when I answered, "That's Katie Morgan . . . My Husband's Wife."

ABOUT THE AUTHOR

New York Times & International Best Selling Author Billie Dureyea Shell was born in Compton California and now lives in Ladera Heights with his wife and kids who he loves to spend time with.

He is the Owner of several properties in the Los Angeles area and gives back to his community by providing low income housing to those who need it.

He stated "It doesn't matter where you at or where you from it's what you do with your time. There's nothing you can't do if you put your mind to it".